THE BLUE MOTH MOTEL

THE
BLUE
MOTH
MOTEL

OLIVIA ROBINSON

BREAKWATER
P.O. Box 2188, St. John's, NL, Canada, A1C 6E6
WWW.BREAKWATERBOOKS.COM

COPYRIGHT © 2021 Olivia Robinson
ISBN 978-1-55081-911-3

We acknowledge the support of the Canada Council for the Arts.
We acknowledge the financial support of the Government of Canada through the
Department of Heritage and the Government of Newfoundland and Labrador
through the Department of Tourism, Culture, Arts and Recreation for our
publishing activities.

PRINTED AND BOUND IN CANADA

Canada Council Conseil des arts
for the Arts   du Canada

Newfoundland
Labrador

Breakwater Books is committed to choosing papers and materials for our
books that help to protect our environment. To this end, this book is printed
on recycled paper that is certified by the Forest Stewardship Council®.

For Emma and Sal
and all those
Prince Edward Island summers

"I shall remember you standing in your blue apron and waving."

– Letter from
Vita Sackville-West to Virginia Woolf,
January 28, 1927

My sister and I lived in a blue motel next to a gas station and the town sewage lagoon. The smell was noticeable only in the height of summer, when it was humid, so when we went outside on those days we breathed through our mouths. The motel was called the Blue Moth because for one night in late June, tiny moths with powdery blue wings swarmed in the grass. But the moths hadn't visited since the 70s, so we treated the story like a myth, another tale conjured by our mother in her constant attempts to make our world more beautiful.

CHAPTER 1

Lewes, UK, 2013

On Wednesday, I lose my voice. The doctor looks like an angler-fish from the deep sea, the one with its own light dangling over the top of its head. But she is not really like a fish at all, with her close-cropped blond hair and efficient manner. She examines my vocal cords through a tube in my nose, which makes it tingle and go numb. It bleeds after she removes the tube and I sit with a tissue pressed to my face while she scribbles in my file.

It's as I suspected, she says as she continues to write. Vocal cord nodules. You'll have to rest for three months, no singing, and speak only when absolutely necessary. Marcia will book you a follow-up appointment.

I had convinced myself, in the couple of months between the initial scratchy feeling in my throat and the increasing hoarseness of my voice, that it was only a persistent cold.

Then what? I say, holding my free hand against my throat.

Well, we might have to consider surgery, the doctor says. She hands me a pad of paper and a golf pencil.

Will I be able to sing again?

I can't promise you anything, she says. But try not to worry too much. No more talking now.

She removes her head mirror and turns off the light. When she spins around on her chair to face me, I notice her bright green eyes and she becomes a creature of the sea again. She doesn't look much older than me, mid-twenties at most, but she must be, and I wonder when in her life she decided to become a doctor or if it was decided for her.

Everything will be fine, the doctor says. I want to ask if anyone ever believes her when she says that, but I refrain. When I moved to the UK at eighteen on a two-year work visa, which has since been extended, it felt like an escape. I know it's a cliché, the desire to leave your younger self behind and become someone different, but if I hadn't left the Blue Moth when I did, it would have held me there in the same way it trapped my sister. Our entire lives were defined by that ramshackle building with its faded blue siding and crumbling swimming pool. I wanted to see something new, be someone new.

But I hadn't realized how hard it is to live on your own. I got a job cleaning Airbnbs and an additional job waiting tables at a pub. I auditioned for church choirs and was accepted into the second one I tried out for. I want to move up to a paid soloist position so I can travel and sing with other choirs, but so far that hasn't worked out. I take private lessons twice a week with a Scottish woman who has a small studio space on the second floor of her flat. We work on my breathing and how I can better position my jaw. Sometimes, on the weekends, I perform a short set in the afternoon at the pub where I work, and get to keep the tips. The thought of having to tell all those people what has happened makes me want to crawl into bed for a week.

Still holding the tissue to my nose, I stand as the doctor opens the door of the examining room. I thank her with a nod of my head and walk down the hallway to the reception area with its green plastic chairs and smell of antiseptic. Marcia, the receptionist, sits behind the desk with a pink cardigan draped over her shoulders. Why is not putting your arms through sleeves a universal indication of sophistication? I avoid eye contact and rush down the stairs out into the fresh early spring air, which holds a hint of rain.

There are palm trees in the south of England. People plant them in their gardens and somehow they survive the winter. This is only one item on a long list of things I have learned about living in the UK, but for some reason it's the one that surprises me most. I had never seen a real palm tree, so seeing one in the garden of a stone cottage with a thatched roof altered my idea of the place. The winters here are different too; the temperature rarely drops below freezing. What would be considered a dusting of snow in Canada is enough to cancel schools and halt traffic.

I rent a room in a house in Lewes, a town I heard of because of Virginia Woolf. The woman who owns the house, Susan, works as a cleaner too. She helped me get the job cleaning the Airbnbs. Every evening when I return home, she is on the soft green sofa in the kitchen with a glass of wine, watching *Strictly Come Dancing* or *Landscape Artist of the Year*. I often join her, accept the offer of a glass of white wine and sit at the table. Susan sips her wine and slowly sinks deeper into the sofa until she drifts off. We don't know each other very well, but on the evenings when she falls asleep on the sofa I put a blanket over her before going upstairs to my room. She looks younger and less tired when she's asleep.

After leaving the doctor's office, all I want to do is sleep. But it's much too early, barely three o'clock, and the bed I'm thinking of isn't the one in my room in Susan's house, but the one I used to share with my older sister, Norah, at the Blue Moth. There's a difference between "a home" and "home"; one is the place you return to most nights, the other is the place to which you feel an obligation. Sometimes they're the same place, but not very often. People try to forget past versions of themselves, but I like to think that pieces of who we were remain in the places we lived, our words lingering in the fabric of the bedroom curtains.

At the post office, a man with a bunch of shiny gold balloons holds the door open for me. As I step past him, he untangles the strings and hands me one.

Tie it around your wrist so it doesn't get away, he says.

Thanks, I say, taking the balloon. When I look up from tying the string, he's already gone.

A single blue envelope sits in my PO box, and I know who it's from before I see the elegant handwriting. Norah is the only person I know who sends mail in powdery blue envelopes. There's only a year between us, and when we were growing up I often felt like the older one, but now Norah has shown her ability to live on her own terms. With the letter in my coat pocket, I leave the post office and walk slowly through the brick court-yard. I feel silly holding the balloon, so I tie it to the back of a bench and walk away.

Having lived in the town for almost three years now, I'm becoming less observant. I used to wander the streets for hours every weekend, staring up at the old buildings for so long people often asked me if I was lost. I spent hours in the antique shops looking at the knick-knacks in their glass cases, flipping through piles of old magazines. Every Saturday, I used to climb the hill to Lewes Castle to take in the view. Now I rush around like everyone else, head ducked against the mist, always somewhere to go. But at this time of the morning the streets are quiet, and I remind myself to look up.

The coffee shop near the train station is empty except for a few older women sitting at a table along the back wall. They each have the same book on the table in front of them, but I can't read the title. I order by pointing at the carafe behind the counter and pay with change. I hold my hand against my throat and grimace, so the woman behind the counter won't think I'm being rude.

I'll bring it to you, she says.

I choose a table by the window, which is fogged up with condensation, and take the envelope out of my pocket. With one finger, I trace the loops of Norah's handwriting and picture her sitting at her kitchen table writing the words. Everything about Norah is beautiful and I envy the calm way she moves through the world. I slip my house key under the flap of the envelope and cut it open, creating a jagged edge I instantly regret. A piece of blue cardstock with gold lettering slides out onto the table:

You are cordially invited to **The Blue Moth Extravaganza!** *The event will take place rain or shine at the Blue Moth Motel on June 21st, 2013. Please RSVP by calling Laurel or Norah.*

Leave it to Norah to resurrect the party of our childhood. The Blue Moth Extravaganza stopped abruptly when I was thirteen. I have no idea why she would want to throw the party again, other than as an excuse to get me home.

The barista brings my coffee in a pale blue mug and sets it on the table in front of me. A woman enters the shop with two children wearing bobble hats and yellow raincoats trotting along behind her. As the woman approaches the counter to place her order, the kids move towards the window near my table and begin drawing with their fingers in the condensation. One makes a smiley face and the other draws a heart. Their fingers squeak against the glass and they giggle at the noise. They draw a few

more shapes before the woman calls them to get their hot chocolate. As I watch, the shapes on the window fill in again with
condensation, but not completely. I can still see the outline of
the heart.

CHAPTER 2

Prince Edward Island, 1990 to 1997

Ingrid and Norah lived at the Blue Moth Motel, in a room they shared with their mother, Laurel. She stuck a red heart on the window so firefighters would know there were kids inside. Laurel was a housekeeper at the motel and their room overlooked the harbour and the city. Only the wide, sloping lawn where the moths supposedly swarmed separated the motel from the water. When Ingrid sat up in bed, she could see the harbour out the side window and the courtyard pool out the main picture window. If she woke up in the middle of the night, she always looked out. The harbour was impenetrable velvet while the pool glowed and pulsed like a jellyfish.

Over the years, the number of tourists who ventured to the Blue Moth began to decline, mainly because of the smell from the sewage lagoon but also because there wasn't much to do on that side of the harbour. Ingrid's grandmother, Ada, had run out of ideas to try and make the place appeal to visitors and was just trying to keep it afloat. Across the water, the city prided itself on its rows of historic brick buildings, waterfront parks, and churches. But summer was a busy season, and if tourists waited too long to book a room in one of the fashionable B & Bs in the city, the Blue Moth was their only option.

Ingrid watched the tourists when they entered the courtyard for the first time and stared up at the neon sign like it was a spaceship. They were mesmerized by the pool, surprised that a place which appeared so plain from the road, with its faded blue vinyl siding and cheap windows, even had a pool. The blue mosaic tiles made the water look tropical, and the palm trees standing next to it appeared to defy the climate but were in fact plastic. By the time the guests entered their rooms and saw the floral wallpaper and green bathroom fixtures, they were convinced of the magic of the Blue Moth and treated it like a place they had discovered on purpose.

Even though she loved living at the Blue Moth, Ingrid wondered what it would be like to live in one of the B & Bs across the harbour. The one on the corner by the library had a weeping willow on the front lawn and a wraparound porch with rocking chairs. Life would be different in a place like that. Rooms with ornate fireplaces and gleaming white walls, sunlight falling through the leaves of the willow onto the polished hardwood floor.

Ada was the owner and manager of the Blue Moth Motel, and Laurel had started working there as a housekeeper when she was sixteen. It was a true family business; Ada had inherited the place from her parents. She lived in a bungalow across town, near a small cove, but was at the motel for most of the day. For the first few years of their lives, Ingrid and Norah barely knew Ada. She was the woman in the office, the person Laurel went to when the washing machines broke or the fridge started leaking. She made the girls feel wary even when she gave them presents for their birthdays and Christmas.

Laurel had moved into one of the motel rooms the summer before her final year of high school. It was a compromise between mother and daughter—Laurel had her space, where Ada could still keep an eye on her. But when Ada learned that Laurel had got pregnant, the arrangement didn't seem so beneficial. For her last three months of high school, Laurel only went in person for tests and exams. Norah arrived in July, a small baby with spidery limbs and a cap of downy blond hair.

Norah and Ingrid's father, Ned, had been in Laurel's class at school. He had sat next to Laurel since middle school, when they used to break pink rubber erasers into chunks and throw them across the room at their classmates. In high school, they smoked cigarettes out behind the soccer field and bought snacks at the convenience store rather than the school cafeteria. There's a photograph of them at their graduation ceremony, arms draped around each other, smiling like they got away with something. The photograph is the only image of Ned and Laurel together, a moment of their lives paused.

That summer and into the fall, Ada let Ned visit Laurel and Norah only once a week, for Friday night supper at the bungalow. The three of them sat around the dining-room table while Norah slept in her car seat in the corner. Ned sat straight and tried to eat slowly as Laurel touched his foot with hers under the table. A weighted blanket of silence hung over the table during those dinners. Ada kept a close eye on her daughter, but she didn't make her move back into the bungalow. In January, Ned left for a job in Alberta and never returned. He sent money and called Laurel on the weekends, but when he learned about Ingrid's forthcoming arrival in the summer, the calls and money stopped.

Rather than track him down, Laurel pretended Ned never existed. It was easier than telling the truth—that she wanted someone to make her feel less lonely, and for a while she had thought that was Ned. But Norah needed her so much more than he did. And so would the new baby. Laurel continued working until Ada made her stop. A guest had expressed concern about "the pregnant young woman delivering the towels," and Laurel was asked to remain in her room, reading novels and crunching ice cubes between her teeth.

Laurel was exhausted all the time. In June 1992, two months before Ingrid was born, Ada hired a new housekeeper to take over Laurel's workload. Elena had vibrant red hair and a loud, contagious laugh that echoed in the courtyard. Her hands waved when she spoke, as if she were conducting an orchestra. She was saving money to attend university and lived in a small apartment across the harbour. The first time she saw Norah, who was almost a year old, Elena lifted the baby into her arms and tossed her into the air. She was an eerily quiet baby, but when Elena tossed her into the air and caught her, Norah screamed with laughter. It was as if her brief moment in the sky woke her up to her own existence, and a couple of weeks later she was trying to talk all the time. She tottered around after Elena, saying nonsense words which Elena replied to as if they were carrying on a conversation. And that was the beginning.

Norah and Ingrid couldn't remember a time without Elena. She wore multicoloured embroidery thread bracelets on her wrists and took pictures of everything. There would be very few baby pictures of the girls if it wasn't for Elena's love for disposable cameras. Even when Ingrid was born, Elena was there holding Laurel's hand, making funny faces and impersonating the doctors when they left the room.

At first, Ada had trouble with Laurel and Elena's relationship.

She was envious of her daughter's carefree nature, the way she didn't seem to mind what other people thought about her. Ada had never felt able to live like that, but the world was different now. Elena gave up her apartment and moved into the room at the Blue Moth with Laurel and the girls. A few doors down, there was a small room with a broken television and cracked bathroom mirror. It wasn't used for guests because of the size, so Laurel and Elena started going there for what they called alone time. Ingrid, as a toddler, would say: Why is it alone time when you go together? Elena was clearly good for Laurel. When one of them was working, the other was looking after Norah and Ingrid. Elena taught the girls how to swim in the courtyard pool when they barely knew how to walk, and Laurel taught them both to read by the time they were four.

On hot evenings in the summer, the four of them drove into the city to get ice cream. Laurel and Elena owned a white Nissan with a useless muffler and no hubcaps. The driver's side door didn't open, so Laurel had to climb in through the passenger seat and over the gearshift to get behind the wheel. She had to push the seat all the way back in order to accommodate her long legs. Then she would sit back with a sigh and slap her palms against the steering wheel. Elena climbed into the passenger seat and they were off. An evergreen-scented air freshener swung back and forth from the rear-view mirror.

It was the summer before the girls were due to start school. Norah was supposed to be enrolled already, but Laurel had held her back a year so she could start at the same time as Ingrid. Norah was shy. She sometimes hid in the narrow space between the bed and nightstand with her chin resting on her knees and her arms wrapped around her shins.

That was also the summer the girls became obsessed with oceans. They huddled together in the middle of the back seat with their seat belts stretched, looking at a library book about starfish. Norah rested her head on Ingrid's shoulder and Laurel clicked the radio on. A Dolly Parton song started playing through the static. Humming along, Ingrid turned the pages of the book only when Norah nodded her head to say she was ready. Elena started singing and Laurel joined in.

The second-best part about going out for ice cream was sitting on the turquoise stools along the shiny counter. They spun around, and Ingrid liked to swing all the way to one side and then let go, so the stool snapped back fast. Her favourite ice cream was mint chip in a waffle cone, the same as Laurel. Chocolate in a cup for Norah so she could eat it with a spoon, and vanilla with rainbow sprinkles for Elena. She cracked the sugar sprinkles between her teeth and grinned to show the girls the rainbow along her gums.

The girls were used to their routine at the Blue Moth. They followed Laurel and Elena around the rooms while they cleaned, keeping each other entertained with silly songs and dances. Norah enjoyed folding the towels; Ingrid wielded the feather duster like a sword. Laurel switched the radio on in every room. During the summer it was slightly busier with tourists, but through the fall and winter the number of guests declined, and Laurel had more free time to work on her own projects. She wanted to give their room a makeover and was inspired by a picture of an old farmhouse in England called Charleston. The artist Vanessa Bell had lived there with her family from 1916 until her death in 1961. Her sister, Virginia Woolf, frequently visited. At the library Laurel found a biography of Vanessa Bell, a doorstop of a book that sat on her bedside table for months.

She read a few chapters aloud to the girls in the evenings and showed them Bell's colourful patterns and soft florals. They learned how Bell and her partners and their children had painted almost everything in the house: elaborate murals on the fireplace surrounds, floral designs around the windows, and scenes on the inside of armoire doors. But Laurel especially liked the geometric pattern in the dining room, which was stencilled directly onto the walls. Since the photograph was in black and white, there was no way to know what colour the design was, but Laurel wanted to put her own spin on it anyway.

Currently their room was wallpapered in faded pink roses, so Laurel came up with the idea to peel it off and paint her own design. Charleston was a work of art, and Laurel wanted to bring some of that beauty into their room at the Blue Moth. Even though the Blue Moth didn't have an elaborate garden or an orchard like Charleston's, the courtyard pool was a kind of pond.

I like how Vanessa lived, Laurel said one evening as she closed the book. She was the quiet centre of everything.

In September, the girls started school and had to adjust to a new routine. The night before their first day, they arranged their toys in different places around the room so in the morning they could determine for certain whether or not they were alive. Stuffed animals Piglet and Eeyore sat in the armchair, two Barbies lounged next to the TV, and an array of small plastic cats paraded across the dresser. In the morning, they discovered that Piglet and Eeyore had climbed into bed with them and the Barbies were sitting in the armchair watching TV. The cats had scattered around the room, under the beds and the mini-fridge, so the girls spent the first ten minutes of the day finding them before Laurel said it was time to get dressed. Elena had to do the morning shift, so she kissed the girls on the top of their heads as she left the room and wished them good luck on their big day.

Laurel dressed them in matching blue overalls and white T-shirts because she had told the school they were twins, even though they didn't look anything alike. She braided Ingrid's dark, curly hair first, wetting it at the temples in an attempt to keep it flat. Norah's light hair was silky, straight, and easy to braid. It rarely tangled, but the chlorine from the pool had tinged the ends green.

With their brown paper bag lunches tucked into their backpacks, the girls set off for the bus stop with Laurel. On the way, they stopped into the gas station to pick out a treat. Ingrid chose a Kinder Surprise and Norah picked a plain Rice Krispies square in its crinkly blue wrapper. The bus stop was down the road from the gas station; Ingrid skipped ahead while Norah stayed back and held Laurel's hand. Laurel was singing her the theme song for the TV show *The Big Comfy Couch*, which the girls watched every afternoon.

At the bus stop, Ingrid took Norah's other hand. When the bus arrived, the girls climbed the giant steps together. Their backpacks were so large they looked like they belonged to much older children. They sat together in the middle of the bus, Norah next to the window so she could look out. She pressed her palm against the glass and waved, her fingers leaving smears. The bus started moving, and after a few seconds Laurel disappeared from view. Norah's face was white and she gripped Ingrid's hand.

Laurel was waiting outside when school let out. She was leaning against the car with her hands in her pockets when Ingrid and Norah emerged through the double doors in a sea of children. The girls were holding hands, but when Norah saw Laurel, she let go of Ingrid and ran. Norah pushed her way through the older kids, who looked like adults compared to her. Laurel crouched down and Norah crashed into her arms.

It wasn't so bad, Ingrid said when she reached them. I had fun.

I have a surprise for you, Laurel said as she stroked Norah's hair. Come on, let's go.

Some of the other parents waiting for their kids in the pick-up line stared at Laurel as she crawled across the passenger seat and gear shift. She banged her knee on the steering wheel, laughed, and turned in her seat to face the girls as they got settled.

I'll get that door fixed someday, Laurel said. Buckle up!

She drove to the hardware store to get supplies for the painting project. They wandered the aisles and collected paintbrushes, rollers, green tape, a roll of butcher paper, and plastic trays. The store had cans of cheap paint; the colours hadn't been mixed in the shades the customers had wanted, but the greens, pinks, greys, purples, and blues were perfect for Laurel's project. She loaded the paint into the trunk, and as they drove away the cans clanked together. Ingrid couldn't wait to dunk her new paintbrush into all those vivid colours.

Laurel stopped at the gas station on the way home and Ingrid climbed into the front seat to get the plastic bag of sunflower seeds out of the glove compartment. There were a few seagulls around the dumpsters and the girls fed them while Laurel filled the tank. As soon as they got out of the car and started throwing seeds, flocks of gulls appeared, swooping in the air above their heads. The language they spoke wasn't like the peaceful, melodic talk of other birds—their voices were loud and frantic. Seeds scattered like confetti and the girls ran in circles, shrieking, trying to avoid getting pooped on. Seagulls squawked and flapped, chasing each other away from the piles of seed.

Back at the Blue Moth, a few tourists were sitting in chairs by the pool, and they watched as Laurel carried paint cans and the girls helped with the bags of rollers, brushes, and sponges. Laurel made microwave macaroni and cheese for supper and the three of them sat cross-legged on the bed and watched the evening news. There was a story about someone who was leaving explosive devices in bags around Charlottetown. Ingrid had overheard Laurel and Ada talking about it over the summer because it had impacted the tourist numbers. It was important to Laurel that the girls know what was going on in the world, and she tried to answer their questions when they didn't understand. When they finished eating, they started peeling off the wallpaper. Laurel stood on a stool with her metal scraper and spray bottle. She sprayed the wallpaper with water and nudged the scraper under the corner near the ceiling. The first piece came off as a sheet, as if the room were shedding its skin.

The room redecoration project turned out to be the perfect distraction for Norah. School made her mind go into overdrive— so many new people she had to talk to, new things she had to learn—and by the time she returned to the Blue Moth she was exhausted and pale. Designing the paintings helped Norah relax. She drew patterns of waves and leaves and flowers on the brown butcher paper with coloured pencils before she dipped her brush into the paint. Using her designs on the paper as a guide, she painted floral motifs on the lampshades, waves and shells on the dresser and bedside tables, playful cats around the edge of the bathroom mirror. She hadn't decided what to paint on the headboards yet, but she let her sister paint the base layer: pale blue for Laurel and Elena's bed and soft green for the girls. In Laurel and Elena's other room, Laurel peeled the wallpaper off and threw away the old television and mirror. She painted the walls a clean, bright white and bought a new mirror shaped like a seashell to hang above the bathroom sink.

Ingrid often got distracted during the project and ran out into the courtyard to make sure she wasn't missing anything. Sometimes she sought out Elena or went to the office to pester Ada. But Norah's concentration never wavered. The moment the girls returned home from school, Norah sat down on the floor with her pencils and the butcher paper and got to work, her back hunched. They worked on the project for months, through the fall and into the beginning of winter. By the time school let out for the holiday break, the room was much brighter. All the small pieces were finished, but the walls were still white and the headboards blank.

The project was put on pause while the Blue Moth was decorated for Christmas. Elena dragged garlands and plastic trees out of the basement below the office and the girls helped her make the place festive. They draped garlands around the pool fence, decorated trees in the office and breakfast room, strung multicoloured lights around the ice machine. Blue lights stretched around the gazebo down by the water. One weekend, the four of them drove out to a wooded area and collected real fir boughs, twigs with red berries, and a tree the same height as Norah. The boughs and twigs they arranged in their room around the television and above the headboards; the tree stood in a bucket of water in the corner. They spent an entire evening stringing popcorn and cranberries to drape around the tree, among white fairy lights. It took twice as much popcorn because Ingrid kept eating hers instead of putting it on the string.

There were never many guests at the motel over the holidays. A few young people, sometimes with families of their own, in the city for Christmas supper with their parents. The kids looked sideways at Ingrid and Norah as their parents shuffled them from room to car, eyeing them up as potential playmates. But they were never there long enough to play. Sometimes older folks stayed for a few days, just to be around other people. Ada cooked a turkey on Christmas Day and everyone staying at the Blue Moth was invited.

That year, Ingrid's confidence was bolstered by a few months of music class at school, and she convinced Norah to sing a few holiday carols during dessert. The girls held hands and stood at the front of the room. Ingrid put an instrumental CD in the player and pressed play. When the music started, Norah's face drained of colour and she let go of Ingrid's hand. Norah turned around so she was facing away from the people and took Ingrid's hand again. They missed the beginning of the song, so Ingrid jumped in to catch up with the music. Norah started singing too, but quietly, her voice bouncing off the window.

Once they had started singing "Silent Night," Ingrid stopped singing. She wanted to hear Norah's voice on its own. It was high and clear, perfectly pitched, but when Norah realized it was her voice alone floating through the room, she gasped and went silent. The music continued and Ingrid looked sideways at her sister. Tears rose in Norah's pale blue eyes, but she stared straight ahead, her shoulders stiff. That was the end of their performance. The girls returned to their seats and Norah ate her pie carefully, using her fork to break off small bites, which she raised to her mouth without looking away from her plate. Laurel and Elena congratulated the girls, told them they sang very well, but Ingrid barely heard them. She was staring at Norah, trying to meet her eye so she could say sorry, even though she wasn't sure if that was how she felt. But Norah didn't look up.

CHAPTER 3

Lewes

Rather than walking home, I wander the streets and look into shop windows. My bag is heavy on my shoulder and I stop under an awning to adjust it. Gentle rain starts; I hear it on the fabric above my head before I notice it on the pavement. My phone chirps and I look at the message without opening it. It's Julia asking how my appointment went. I slip the phone back into my pocket without replying. Across the street, the glowing windows of a bookshop draw me in.

I'm the only customer. A man sits behind an antique desk and glances up when I enter. He has small round glasses perched on his nose and a green wool toque that doesn't cover his ears. I begin browsing the crowded shelves while he continues to read a tattered paperback. He has the cover folded back on itself so I can't see the title. The shop sells used books and smells like dust and old paper. I like bookshops because they remind me of Norah.

Looks like it's bucketing down out there, the man says. I nod and pick up a paperback copy of an Elizabeth Bowen novel. When he sees me reading the back of it, he stands and approaches. You like Irish writers?

I nod again. I take my phone out of my pocket and open the Notes app to type a message.

– *Can't speak, vocal cord problems.*

He reads the message and looks at me, unsure how to respond. I shrug and try to appear nonchalant about it.

I'm sorry, he says finally. That must be really hard. He rubs his shoulder with one hand and looks down at the floor, then takes a step back. Is it contagious?

I snort and he takes another step back, eyes wide. I shake my head, type a note which explains I'm a singer, and hold it up so he can read it. Even so, he still looks skeptical.

Well, let me know if you need anything, he says as he makes his way back to the desk and picks up his book again.

I browse for a few more minutes before I slip out of the store. The man doesn't look up as I leave. But he was right about the rain—it's pouring now, and I don't have an umbrella. I glance back into the window of the bookshop and pretend Norah is behind the desk. I check my phone and calculate what time it is on Prince Edward Island—two in the afternoon. She would still be at work, probably behind the desk at the bookshop. Customers leave with more books than they intended to buy when Norah is working. She lives in a small apartment above the shop, just her and the cat. When we speak on the phone, she seems happy and busy. Along the wall in her living room, she's built floor-to-ceiling bookshelves.

Standing under the awning outside the bookshop, I pretend Norah is here with me. What would we talk about? Plane tickets are too expensive for anyone to come visit me, and I've only been home once, the first Christmas after I moved away. I miss the Prince Edward Island beaches in the summer, how the warm breeze creates small tornadoes of sand. Walking for hours along the sandbars with Norah, talking and singing verses from random songs. Am I still that person? It's hard to keep track of all the people I used to be.

On the walk home, I steady myself against the buildings when a car whooshes by in the narrow lane. The light is on in the kitchen when I turn onto my street, and I can see Susan's shadow moving behind the blinds. Behind me, people enter the pub, their voices loud with beer. When the door swings open, I hear a few notes of fiddle music and raised voices before it closes. People stand in groups outside, and the smell of cigarettes hits the back of my throat. I cross the street and unlock the front door, finally wishing for silence.

CHAPTER 4

Prince Edward Island, 1998

At school, Norah and Ingrid kept to themselves. In art class they were given an assignment to draw their house and family, so they both drew the Blue Moth. Five people stood on the front lawn underneath the neon sign, their names carefully printed underneath: Ingrid, Norah, Laurel, Elena, and Ada. The teacher, Mrs. Campbell, was impressed by Norah's printing and held the picture up in front of the class as an example. When all the pictures were finished, she taped them on the wall so everyone could take turns looking at them. Ingrid noticed the bungalows and townhouses, a few old farmhouses and one or two apartment buildings, a mom and a dad holding hands.

Ingrid loved the smell of the library and the fact that they got to go there for an hour every day. Ms. Beech, the librarian, read aloud to the class. She held the book up so everyone could see the pictures. There were soft cushions on the floor and rows of tall wooden bookshelves. The books were covered in plastic and crinkled when they were opened. Some of the pages were stained with the fingerprints of previous readers.

For the rest of the winter, the girls worked on the redecoration project after school, sometimes on their own and sometimes with help from Laurel or Elena. Even though it was cold outside, inside their room at the Blue Moth, the world was bright and floral and smelled of paint. In the evenings, Elena helped them with their homework and read them a story before bed. Elena made sure each character in the book had a different voice, and she made funny sound effects.

Their most requested bedtime story, however, wasn't in a book. It was the story of the blue moths, recited by Laurel in hushed tones with the lights out, like a ghost story. The story started in the past, when the Blue Moth Motel was first built by Laurel's great-grandmother, Miranda, who was a witch. She ran the place with two of her friends from childhood, who were also witches, and they lived in a small cottage down by the water where the gazebo now stood. They were the first to see the moths, one evening on the summer solstice, which became the first Blue Moth Extravaganza. And the moths were ghostlike; they appeared out of nowhere, fluttering in the grass for a few moments before they disappeared.

The moths appeared at dusk, Laurel said, her voice raspy and quiet. The three friends were having a bonfire, as they did every year to welcome the summer, standing around the flames as they crackled and leapt into the air. The sky faded to a soft lilac as the sun disappeared, and that was when Miranda noticed the moths.

Laurel paused at this point in the story. She let the scene sink in, waited until Ingrid grabbed her arm and asked her to continue. There were freckles on Laurel's arms and across her cheeks which reminded Ingrid of constellations and she often wondered if her mother was a witch, too.

Suddenly, all around their feet, tiny blue moths appeared, Laurel said. Miranda didn't understand what was happening because they had appeared from nowhere, as if they had come up through the earth itself. And then, just as quickly, they rose up towards the lilac sky. Wings brushed against Miranda's legs, arms, and cheeks, and she closed her eyes. When she opened them, the moths were gone and the sky was dark. The only way she knew the moths were real was the iridescent blue powder which coated her clothes and skin.

What happened next? Norah said, even though she knew.

The next year, Miranda and her friends held another Blue Moth Extravaganza, Laurel continued. This time, they invited everyone who was staying at the Blue Moth, as well as some of their friends from the city. They told everyone about the magical moths, lit the bonfire, and waited eagerly for them to appear.

But they didn't come! Ingrid jumped in.

Don't ruin the story! Norah nudged Ingrid with her foot under the blankets.

They waited and waited, Laurel said, but as the sky got darker, the moths didn't appear. The guests still had a good time and most of them had forgotten about the moths anyway. But Miranda couldn't figure out why they hadn't reappeared. She thought about it for a long time, did research, but nothing conclusive emerged. After a year of thinking and reading, Miranda decided that only she and her two friends would attend the next Blue Moth Extravaganza. So once again, they lit the bonfire and stood around it as the sun set. And when the sky turned purple, the moths appeared and covered the women in the same iridescent blue powder, before they flew away into the sky.

But why did it happen? Ingrid asked. Are the moths shy, like Norah?

Laurel started to speak, but then Norah sat up in bed.

I know why, Norah said. Everyone around the fire has to believe in the moths or else they won't appear. When the witches invited all those people, the moths knew there were some people who didn't believe in them. So they didn't appear.

Maybe that's why we haven't seen them, Ingrid said. We need to have a Blue Moth Extravaganza! If we have a big party, we can find out if that's the reason the moths didn't arrive! Can we have one this summer?

I don't see why not, Laurel said. Now, time to go to sleep.

───────

Laurel and Elena took turns walking the girls to the bus stop, but on Fridays the four of them walked together. The crusty remains of snowbanks lined the road as spring arrived. A few weeks before school ended for the year, Norah designed a poster for The Blue Moth Extravaganza. She drew a large, detailed blue moth and Elena wrote the date, time, and location underneath the wings. Ingrid sat cross-legged on their bed and watched Norah lying on her stomach on the floor with coloured pencils scattered around. Norah bit her lip when she concentrated and sometimes made it bleed.

When the poster was finished, Laurel drove the girls into the city to the big public library to make copies. Each colour copy cost ten cents, so they made twenty-five copies, which Norah placed carefully in a plastic folder she clutched against her chest. They put one poster up on the bulletin board at the library and stuck a few on telephone poles downtown. They left a few copies at the gas station and in the breakfast room and main office at the Blue Moth. Norah saved one copy for herself and taped it to the wall by her side of the bed.

The day before the party, Norah and Ingrid helped Laurel and Elena clean the rooms so they could start decorating. At the dollar store, they bought balloons, streamers, confetti, and paper lanterns to hang in the gazebo. Almost all of the guests at the Blue Moth had complimented Norah on her poster design and said they would definitely attend the party. The girls collected dirty towels and left clean ones, distributed mini shampoos and bars of soap wrapped in paper, and made sure everyone knew about The Blue Moth Extravaganza.

Around mid-afternoon, a truck pulled into the courtyard outside the office. Ingrid was standing outside one of the rooms with the towel cart. Inside, Norah was arranging the clean linens. The truck backed up close to the door of the breakfast room and two men in overalls got out. Norah emerged from the room and stood next to Ingrid; they watched as the men unrolled a ramp from the back and disappeared inside. A few moments later, something large covered by a dark sheet emerged from the back of the truck and the men carefully manoeuvred it down the ramp. Ada appeared in the doorway of the office. She had a colourful scarf wrapped around her curly, bobbed grey hair and when she noticed the girls across the courtyard, she waved. Ingrid waved back, confused, as Ada went over to talk to the men.

What do you think it is? Norah asked, as the three adults and the strange object disappeared into the breakfast room. They crossed the courtyard and hovered outside the door, peeking around the door frame. The delivery men removed the dark sheet and revealed a piano.

That night, Norah and Ingrid woke up at midnight and snuck out of their room. Laurel and Elena slept soundly, cocooned in blankets, but the girls tiptoed anyway and left the door open a crack. The pool, open for the season, gurgled away, emitting its blue glow. Silhouetted against the dark sky, the palm trees looked very real. All the rooms were in darkness, their occupants sound asleep. But across the courtyard, a single light glowed in the breakfast room.

The girls slowly walked around the perimeter of the pool and as they neared the breakfast room, they heard the music. Ingrid grabbed Norah's arm and they both stopped and listened. The notes floated across the pool and the girls froze. Since they couldn't see the piano, the music had a ghostly quality. Ingrid started walking again first, and Norah followed. They crept closer to the breakfast room and crouched down under the windows. Slowly, they lifted their heads to peer inside.

The upright piano, like the one in the music room at school, stood against the back wall. Ada was sitting on the bench, her face and hands illuminated by a small light on top of the piano. She was wearing a long blue dressing gown that draped over the back of the bench like liquid. Ingrid had thought her grandmother was an old woman, but as she watched her play, she realized she wasn't that old after all. She looked elegant and serene, her face less pinched than usual. The girls crawled to the open door and sat. They were afraid of being seen but didn't want to go back to bed. Norah rested her head on Ingrid's shoulder and closed her eyes.

On the morning of the party, Laurel, Elena, Ingrid, and Norah drove to the beach. They packed hard-boiled eggs and juice boxes in a small cooler that Elena carried over her shoulder. Laurel was the type of person who believed boiling an egg counted as cooking. The girls swam until the skin on their fingers and toes wrinkled and their eyes stung from the salt. Laurel and Elena collected driftwood for the bonfire later and took turns reading aloud to each other while keeping an eye on Ingrid and Norah. When the girls got hungry, they ran back to their towels and dripped their wet hair onto Laurel and Elena's legs, making them shriek and chase the girls down the beach.

Ingrid took the eggs out of the cooler and peeled hers. Against the red sand, the white shells looked like vibrant drops of paint. She ate her egg in two bites and tucked the halves into the sides of her mouth so her cheeks bulged. Sand always ended up on the eggs, but it made them taste salty so no one minded the crunch.

The girls couldn't remember a time when they didn't know how to swim. They raced each other and had contests to see who could hold their breath the longest underwater. The pool was their first watery home, but they were also in love with the wildness of the ocean. Jumping over the frothy breakers, Ingrid and Norah swam out and let the waves carry them back to shore, depositing them on the sand like shells. Over and over they threw themselves into the surf and let it bring them back until the sun started getting low in the sky and it was time to go home for the party.

The blue streamers tied around the pool fence were fluttering in the wind when they arrived back at the Blue Moth. Ingrid and Norah ran and tied balloons outside the door to every room and set up a trail of battery-operated tea lights to lead the way down to the gazebo, where Laurel stood on a stepladder and hung dozens of paper lanterns from the wooden beams. Elena stood behind her, spotting.

Once the paper lanterns were in place, Elena started the bonfire in a circle of rocks. The air smelled like pine and smoke.

Norah and Ingrid went to their room and changed into their matching blue plaid dresses. Their hair was crusty with salt, and Ingrid's curls were tangled and wild around her face. The girls ran barefoot along the tea light trail and chased each other around the bonfire.

Guests started to arrive, carrying blankets and folding chairs under their arms. They chose their spot by the bonfire or milled around talking, drinking beer. In the dusk, everyone looked more like themselves. Laurel had bought a pack of sparklers from the gas station and she lit the first ones now for Ingrid and Norah. They held the long sticks and kept running, waving them in circles to watch the sparks leap and fade. As the fire moved closer to Ingrid's fingers, she wondered if it would hurt. But a few inches before the end of the stick, the spark went out.

Elena arranged the food and roasting sticks on a picnic table and people started cooking food over the coals. Someone brought a boom box and put on a CD of old country songs in the gazebo. As the sun started to set, more people arrived with beer and with wood to toss on the fire. Old apple crates broken into pieces, wooden pallets, and driftwood from the beach all ended up in the blaze. Each time someone threw a new piece of wood on, the flames shot into the air like a hungry creature happy to be fed. The girls spun with their sparklers and Ingrid wished they wouldn't fade so quickly. Distracted by their activities, the girls didn't notice Ada. She knew about the party from the posters hanging all around the motel, but no one thought she would attend. The last Blue Moth Extravaganza had taken place when Ada was young, shortly before her mother died.

Norah saw Ada first and grabbed Ingrid's arm. Ada carried a wine bottle in one hand and was wearing a long, flowing blue chiffon dress which billowed out behind her. Norah stepped forward and handed her a lit sparkler.

Thank you, Ada said. Any sign of the moths?

Ingrid had forgotten all about the moths in the excitement of the sparklers and staying up past bedtime. But seeing Ada brought the story back to life. She held the sparkler up close to her face.

No moths yet, Norah said. She stepped close to Ada and touched her long chiffon sleeve. I like your dress.

Well, let's go down closer to the water to see if we can find them, Ada said.

She set the bottle of wine down on the picnic table and took Norah's hand. Ingrid followed along behind. They stopped a few feet away from the edge of the grass, where the crumbling sandstone bank gave way to a sliver of beach below. People used to swim here, but now the harbour was too polluted, and the girls were only allowed to step onto the beach if they were wearing shoes. Broken beer bottles littered the sand, along with razor clams and purple mussel shells.

Ada sat down in the grass and leaned back on her hands to look up at the sky. A few stars blinked to life. Ingrid watched as Norah sat down next to their grandmother, so Ingrid did the same.

Now we wait, Ada said.

The moths didn't come, but the girls sat with Ada for a long time, looking up at the sky and down in the grass, searching for a glimpse of iridescent blue wings. Ingrid listened to the gentle lapping of waves against the sand, the crackling fire, the hum of music and voices. She tried to be patient, but it was hard sitting still. On the other side of Ada, Norah was quiet, her chin tilted up.

Laurel approached the three of them and put her hand on Ingrid's shoulder.

Do you want to make s'mores? Laurel said. It's getting late.

Yes! Ingrid said, jumping to her feet. Norah shook her head. I'm going to stay here, she said. The moths might still show up.

Ingrid followed her mother back to the fire and put a marshmallow on a stick. She glanced down to the water where Norah and Ada still sat, two shadows just visible against the lights across the harbour. In the fire, the marshmallow went up in flames and fell off the stick into the coals.

By ten o'clock, the party was starting to wind down. Ingrid had eaten too many marshmallows and felt slightly sick. Down by the water, Norah had fallen asleep in the grass. Ada lifted the girl into her arms and carried her towards the group at the fire.

I think it's time for bed, she said.

During her brief life so far, Ingrid couldn't remember Ada ever tucking them into bed at night. Ada usually left the Blue Moth shortly after suppertime and returned to her bungalow across town. But something about her was different tonight, and Ingrid thought it might have to do with the piano. She followed Ada and Norah along the tea-light path back to the Blue Moth. Ada's dress billowed out behind her and made it look like she could take flight at any moment. To Ingrid, her grandmother seemed both young and old, and she wasn't sure how that could be. All she knew was that something felt different, a nearly imperceptible change in the wind.

CHAPTER 5

Lewes

At midnight on Friday, people spill out of the pub across the street. My room is at the back of the house, but the way voices echo across the narrow street makes it sound like there's a party in the back garden. I get out of bed and sit at my desk by the window, leaning my chin in my hands. The desktop is covered in sheet music for the songs I'm supposed to be learning before choir practice on Sunday. I glance at the notes; in my head I hear everyone's voices floating up to the ceiling of the church. In a strange way, the raised voices of the drunk pub-goers resemble a choir. Deep voices blending with higher ones, the occasional puncture of laughter. It's less transcendent but holds a certain degree of beauty if you listen closely.

I can spend an entire afternoon sitting at my desk and looking down into the back gardens of the other houses, all those other worlds. Susan's is full of terracotta pots waiting to be planted. In the spring, she spends every moment of her free time out there tending to the flowers and when she comes back in she brings the smell of earth and hot sun. A small tree climbs the stone wall at the back of the garden, where birds nestle among the leaves and chirp. I enjoy the contrast of stone and brick; the tall chimneys rising up remind me of that scene in *Mary Poppins* when the chimney sweeps do their dance. Norah and I had a VHS copy of *Mary Poppins* that we played so many times we broke the tape.

I collect up all the loose sheet music and tuck it away in my desk drawer so I don't have to look at it. I reach for the cellphone on my bedside table and text the choir director, Julia, who also happens to be my girlfriend. No one else in the choir knows we're together, and part of me wonders if our relationship is responsible for me not getting promoted to soloist. Julia is twenty-nine and it's still a mystery what she sees in me, but we've been together almost a year. She texts me back almost immediately even though it's late. I pull on a sweater and creep out of the house. Once I'm outside, I pull the thick curtain back across before I close the door and lock it. Susan's house is old and drafty, so she has a curtain hanging inside the front door to keep out the damp. It was a practice new to me, but Susan told me it's common in the UK.

The pub-goers are too busy talking and smoking to notice me as I start down the street in the direction of the river. Julia lives in a small apartment a ten-minute walk from my place. The apartment is on the top floor of a house but has its own entrance through the back garden. The couple Julia rents from also let her use the small shed in the garden for her pottery. Other than the sounds of people clustered outside the pubs, the streets are quiet. When I arrive, Julia is standing in the doorway. I must look worse than I thought, because when she sees me, her brows furrow and she opens the door wide.

I explain everything through text messages. Julia makes tea in a green ceramic pot she threw herself and pours it into two matching mugs that she also made. The mugs have a freckled appearance; they look rough but feel surprisingly smooth. They are Julia in mug form. I hold mine close to my face to breathe in the steam.

It's okay, Julia says. You can take a break from the choir until you're better. And you don't have to talk to clean, so you can still do one of your jobs.

I'm grateful for her not asking why I ignored her earlier text and for reminding me of the things I can still do. But with only one job I'll go broke within a month, and the possibility of never being able to sing again makes my chest feel tight. Who will I be without my voice? I don't want Julia to ask me the other question I've been rolling over and over in my mind like a pebble. If I can't sing and can't work, will I have to return to the Blue Moth?

Let's go to bed, Julia says. Her apartment is warm and smells of cinnamon. I look at her, really look, for the first time since I arrived. She's wearing floral print pajamas which have shrunk in the dryer and her strawberry blond hair hangs over her shoulder in a loose braid. Her feet are bare on the carpet and there's mascara smudged around her eyes. The purple shadows underneath make me realize my text woke her up, and she got up to answer it.

I take off my sweater and crawl under the soft green duvet. Julia takes the tea things back to the kitchen area and I hear the fridge door open, the rustle of a plastic bag. As she climbs into bed, she presses something cold against my back and I gasp and turn over to glare at her. But it's impossible to be angry as she holds up the McIntosh apple and takes a bite. She only likes apples that are crisp and cold even though they make her teeth hurt. I stifle a laugh and it comes out through my nose more like a squeak as I roll over and press my face against the duvet. With her back against the headboard, Julia reaches for a book on her bedside table. I drift off curled up on one side, listening to her turn the pages.

CHAPTER 6

Prince Edward Island, 1998 to 1999

For the rest of the summer after The Blue Moth Extravaganza, the girls continued their painting project. Norah drew a geometric pattern with circles and triangles, and she and Ingrid used sponges to press the paint onto the walls. Laurel had decided not to tell Ada about the redecoration. The colours and patterns made the room resemble a colouring book being carefully filled in. It looked bigger without the oppressive pink floral wallpaper, and the designs on the lampshades made the lighting softer and more golden. It was small potatoes compared to the extensive beauty of Charleston, the farmhouse in Sussex where Vanessa Bell lived, but the girls were happy with the little world they created in their room.

Guests were still on the decline that summer. More cottages were being built out closer to the nice beaches, so fewer tourists were staying in the city. Ada spent her days on the phone in the office, placing ads in local newspapers, updating the website, and trying to get the unique appeal of the Blue Moth Motel across to people who hadn't already stumbled on it. Even though it was only a five-minute drive into the city and the skyline was visible from the Blue Moth, the motel didn't have enough amenities to draw people in. Tourists were searching for quaint cottages with ocean views, proximity to the water parks and picturesque walking trails. An ancient motel next to a gas station and sewage lagoon, with a beach too small for sunbathing, and with water too polluted to swim in, wasn't even on their list.

Sometimes, at night, Norah and Ingrid snuck out of their bed and went to the breakfast room to look at the piano. This was the year they first watched *Mary Poppins*, and they sang the songs over and over all day. In the breakfast room, they didn't turn on the light. Norah sat on the piano bench and softly ran her fingers over the keys. She pretended to play while Ingrid sat on the bench beside her and sang "Stay Awake" from *Mary Poppins* as quietly as possible.

Since there was less work to do at the Blue Moth, Laurel took an additional job tending the cemetery at a small church near Ada's bungalow. The building overlooked a beach; a path led from the cemetery to the sand. Once a week, Laurel drove out there and mowed the grass, watered the rose bushes, washed the windows, and weeded around the headstones. She wore knee pads and purple garden gloves. The girls came with her for the adventure and hid among the trees and headstones, jumping out to scare each other. That summer they were turning six and seven, just old enough to understand the concept of death. When she thought about the people lying under the ground in the dark, Ingrid ran faster. Since the beach was secluded and small, it was unknown and undesirable to tourists; there was room to run there too.

A large tree trunk jutting out of the sandstone bank became a pretend surfboard. Ingrid and Norah took turns lying on their stomachs on the rough bark, pretending to paddle out into the waves. While Norah jumped up into a surfing position, Ingrid stood nearby and pretended to be the announcer, using a stick as a microphone. Then they switched spots. At first, they fell off the tree a lot, scraping their legs and arms against the branches. But after a month or so of practice, their balance improved, and they rarely fell.

Another favourite game was Around the World. In the office at the Blue Moth, there was a globe on Ada's desk. She let them play with the globe to keep them occupied. They took turns spinning it with their eyes closed and one finger resting lightly on the globe. When it stopped spinning, the place where your finger landed was where you were supposed to travel. Norah kept track of the destinations in a notebook. If they landed in the middle of the ocean, it meant they had to swim in that ocean and could choose which coastline to access it from.

On the weekends, Laurel and Elena took the girls to the neighbourhood library. They could walk there in a few minutes. They looked at books about Athens, Budapest, Ireland, and the Indian Ocean. The library smelled like musty books and old carpet and crayons. Older people answered their emails and played solitaire on the computers. The small, white building was more like a house than a library. The girls checked out every book about faraway destinations and read about the people and animals who lived there. Ingrid was drawn to the blue-and-white stucco buildings of Santorini, Norah to Egypt and the unexplored tombs. They wanted to see everything, to explore exciting places and send postcards back to Laurel and Elena from every city in the world.

After the library, they often went to the grocery store. Norah and Ingrid took turns pushing the cart. If a good song came on over the speakers, anything by ABBA, Cher, or Cyndi Lauper, Ingrid started dancing. Other shoppers stared at her as she sashayed down the aisles. Once, while doing a funny two-step, she accidentally knocked into a display of pasta sauce with the cart. It toppled, and the glass bottles shattered, coating the linoleum floor in a sloppy mess. Laurel grabbed a mop and bucket which she found unattended near the swinging door that led into the store's back room. But the water only pushed the sauce around, creating a red puddle, so she flagged down an employee for help.

The Blue Moth was still barely breaking even the following summer, so Laurel kept her job at the cemetery and started cleaning inside the church as well. She mopped the floors, dusted the pews, straightened the hymn books, and changed light bulbs. The girls often met up with her there after school and did their homework in the pews. Ingrid's voice echoed in the space, even when she spoke at a regular volume.

When school let out for the year and the weather got warmer, the girls spent more time on the beach. Elena joined them and sat in a low beach chair, soaking up the sun. Her college plans were on hold and she was still working at the Blue Moth. The girls had an inflatable raft tied to a rope so they could float on the water but not drift too far from shore. They pretended to be on a ship at sea, setting out for new adventures. One end of the rope was tethered to Elena's beach chair.

Norah went out on the raft alone one afternoon because Ingrid wanted to stay on the beach reading a book about two friends in an art gallery. When she looked up from the book, the raft was a yellow dot against the blue. The rope had come loose. Elena was asleep, her head tilted back. Ingrid shook her awake and Elena's eyes blinked open, squinting against the sun. She raised a hand above her eyes and when she saw Ingrid's face she leapt to her feet, swore loudly, and ran into the waves.

Ingrid turned and ran in the opposite direction, back up the path to the church to get Laurel, who went into the office to call Search and Rescue. The tile was cold under Ingrid's feet and goosebumps rose on her arms and legs. Standing in the middle of the aisle in her bathing suit, she felt small and alone.

Laurel burst out of the office, grabbed Ingrid's hand, and ran back down to the beach. They scanned the water for Elena and the raft, but they couldn't be seen anymore. Laurel yelled for Elena and Norah. The wind snatched her voice and carried it down the beach.

They stood at the water's edge, the waves licking their toes, until they heard the rumble of tires on sand. The Search and Rescue crew backed a truck into the waves and unloaded a Jet Ski. Someone in a red bathing suit and a bright orange life vest jumped on board and shot off towards the horizon. Another crew member asked Laurel questions. Ingrid answered most of them while Laurel stared out to sea, following the spout of water.

A short time later, the Jet Ski returned with Elena and Norah on the back and the small raft, half deflated, being towed along behind. Elena's eyes were red, her face pale, but Norah looked strangely calm. She was sitting between Elena and her rescuer, hands clenched on the straps of the rescuer's life jacket. Her own life jacket was a bit too big and hid her neck. The Jet Ski drove up on the sand and Laurel ran to Norah and scooped her up into her arms even though she was almost too big for Laurel to lift. Elena climbed off the Jet Ski, but her steps were uncertain. Slowly, she lowered herself to the sand and sat with one arm braced against the ground to keep herself upright.

Ingrid moved towards Elena and sat down next to her. The crew lingered, asked to check vitals and provided information about water safety. Once they were satisfied that everyone was fine, they loaded the Jet Ski back onto the truck and drove away. The tire tracks looked wrong against the sand, their sharp edges too clearly defined.

Back at the Blue Moth that evening, before they fell asleep, Ingrid asked Norah if she had been scared out there on the raft, all alone in the middle of the ocean. Elena and Laurel were out by the pool, sitting with their feet in the water. They were leaning against each other, creating a single shadow on the surface of the pool. In the dim blue light of the bedroom, Norah rolled over to face Ingrid.

No, I wasn't scared, she said. The wind sounded like music.

The girls weren't allowed on the beach for a while after that. When Laurel went to work at the church, they stayed at the Blue Moth with Elena. She taught them how to make embroidery thread bracelets and they showed her how to play Around the World. They watched movies and learned the songs in every soundtrack. Ingrid belted the lyrics into a hairbrush and jumped up and down on the bed.

In the evenings when Laurel came home, the four of them swam in the pool and then went to get ice cream in their bathing suits, leaving water stains on the seat of the Nissan. People at the ice cream shop sometimes stared, and at first Ingrid thought it was because she and Norah were wearing bathing suits. But they were staring at Laurel and Elena, who were holding hands. The four of them sat along the counter like they always had, and Ingrid spun back and forth on her stool.

One evening, the girls woke up to the sound of music. They stared at each other in the near-darkness and listened, then slipped out of bed and went to investigate. Once they were out in the courtyard, Norah recognized the song from music class.

It's "*Für Elise*," she said.

Ingrid hovered in the doorway, but Norah walked straight into the breakfast room. Ingrid said Norah's name under her breath, but Norah didn't turn around. She walked over to the piano bench and sat down next to Ada in the pool of light. Norah watched Ada's hands, and when the song was finished, Ada guided Norah's hands onto the keys.

She didn't play perfectly, but considering that she'd never actually played a piano before, she seemed to catch on instantly. It was as if she had learned a language by listening and now had to figure out how to write it down. Ada guided her through a few easy songs, starting with "Hot Cross Buns" and "Happy Birthday" before showing her a slowed-down version of "*Für Elise*." When Norah heard the familiar notes, she tried to play faster. She hit a few incorrect keys, but rather than getting flustered, she paused for a moment and began again. Ingrid watched Ada put one arm around Norah's shoulders, and something seemed to shift almost imperceptibly, like a glass door sliding closed. Norah had gone somewhere else; from then on, Ingrid would always feel she was running to catch up.

When fall came, the girls ran from the bus stop every day after school, threw their backpacks in their room, and raced across the courtyard to the breakfast room. Ada was waiting with apple slices and cubes of cheese on small plates. The girls ate their snack and listened to Ada play.

Once she had finished eating, Norah sat next to Ada on the piano bench and ran through scales. She caught on faster than Ingrid did and found it easier to read the music. For Ingrid, the notes remained jumbled together on the lines. But she remembered lyrics more easily than Norah and could sing a song back after hearing it only once or twice.

Ada taught them beginner songs and exercises to warm up their vocal cords. Ingrid's favourite one was high-pitched humming while buzzing her lips, because it made them feel fuzzy. After an hour or so, Ingrid was eager to escape. She wanted to swim or go down to the gazebo to see if there were any ships in the harbour. But Norah would sit on that piano bench forever.

Norah found a long piece of cardboard, which she used to make a pretend keyboard. Using a permanent marker, she drew the outline of the keys and shaded in the black ones. She put the keyboard on top of the dresser, stood in front of it, and pretended to play. Ingrid hummed the notes under her breath to help, but after a few minutes Norah told her to stop.

I can hear them in my head, she said.

Ada realized Ingrid got bored faster than Norah and started bringing books to keep Ingrid occupied while Norah practised: *Little Women, The Wind in the Willows, The Secret Garden,* and *Little House on the Prairie.* Ingrid wanted to learn how to play, but she lacked patience. Singing, by contrast, seemed like instant gratification. Ingrid liked to make her voice do different things, go from loud to soft and back again. Rather than figuring out what her real voice sounded like, she tried to impersonate other singers. Her voice twanged and trilled; she tried to understand Julie Andrews' four-octave range and attempted to imitate it. As Ingrid learned to sing, she was convinced she would be the best.

CHAPTER 7

Lewes

Julia rises early, so I often wake up alone. It's Saturday morning—
I'm supposed to be at the pub by three for the evening shift and
it's almost noon. I pull the duvet up over my head and groan as
I remember yesterday and feel the familiar ache in my throat.

Are you awake? Julia says from the doorway. I pull the duvet
away and sit up against the pillows. Julia is wearing her long grey
pottery apron and there are flecks of red clay on her cheeks and
in her hair. She leans against the door frame.

Take your time, Julia says. I called Nina at the pub and told
her you're sick today, so you have the weekend to figure out what
you want to do. I'm almost done in the shed, so we can go for
breakfast soon, yeah? At that place by the river?

Julia leaves the door ajar when she slips out again. I climb out
of bed. A square of sun falls through the window onto the carpet,

and I stretch my arms over my head. The idea of an entire day without anything to do makes me restless. I cross the room to the bedroom window, which overlooks the street. The window has a wide sill and I can smell the damp earth and the river. I want to swim, but it's still too cold; the freshwater pool, the Pells, isn't open yet for the season. On the pavement below, a teenager walks a beagle on a leash, tugging the dog along when he tries to stop and smell a bench. A woman wearing a red beret hurries out of a clothing store, her arms laden with bags. Sometimes I try to picture what each person's house might look like, if they're married, if they have pets. I watch the dog walkers, to see if each dog matches up with their human.

Julia's bathroom is full of plants: ferns in large ceramic pots and succulents dripping from shelves. Moisture-loving plants which collect the steam on their leaves and make small puddles on the floor. She told me they remind her of Australia, where she went to university. I almost slip as I step out of the shower but grab the towel bar. Pots clatter in the kitchen as I wrap a towel around my hair and dash across the short hallway into the bedroom.

You left wet footprints on the carpet again! Julia calls from the hallway.

I ignore her, pull on my clothes from yesterday, and text Susan. The house is so small we know each other's schedules by the swish of the front door curtain, the dishes in the sink, footsteps on the stairs.

Half an hour later, Julia and I finally leave on our quest for breakfast. As she locks the door, I walk to the corner to wait for her. Painted on the side of the white stone building across the road, there's a Mary Poppins figure. The image is about halfway up the side of the building and shows the turned-out feet, the carpet bag, and the umbrella for which Mary Poppins is most well-known. But the umbrella is inside out and I'm not sure how it's lifting her into the sky.

Julia appears by my side and puts her arm around my waist. We browse the antique shops along the High Street. Julia enjoys looking at all the bric-a-brac, especially old pottery, but I find the shops a bit claustrophobic. All those old items, arranged together in large quantities, remind me too much of death. But I try to absorb some of Julia's excitement and listen as she explains potter's marks and the difficulties of terracotta.

We sit at a table by the window and study the menus. When the server returns, Julia orders for me. We both get eggs benedict, no meat, orange juice, and coffee. It's difficult to have a conversation when one of the people participating isn't supposed to speak, but Julia tries to ask yes or no questions to make it easier. When the food arrives, we eat in silence.

CHAPTER 8

Prince Edward Island, 2000 to 2002

Ingrid memorized every song from the *Mary Poppins* soundtrack to *The Sound of Music*. She was still trying to imitate Julie Andrews, with little success. Slowly, with Norah's help, Ingrid also learned how to read music. The girls borrowed songbooks from the library and sat side by side on the piano bench in the breakfast room, Norah playing while Ingrid sang. Ada taught them every day after school, but by suppertime she had to go home. The piano faced the wall, so when they sat on the bench they had their backs to the room. If anyone clapped or came over and complimented Norah on her playing, her face flushed and she stopped. As long as she didn't have to see or speak to anyone, Norah would play forever, but as soon as someone spoke, the magic was broken. The girls returned to their room, where Norah sat cross-legged on the floor with a piece of plywood over her knees, still refining the designs for the head-boards. Something in Norah had changed after the incident at the beach. She was still shy, reluctant to speak at school, but when she looked at Ingrid there was something different behind Norah's eyes, a new sense of determination.

At school, the girls learned to play the recorder, and during recess and lunch the music teacher let them practise on the piano in the music room. They didn't make any friends because they stayed indoors while everyone else went outside to play. The other kids thought Ingrid and Norah were strange because of their reluctance to swing on the monkey bars or go down the slide. The girls became the source of much speculation at school. Their classmates knew they lived in a motel and sometimes the other kids stared at Ingrid and Norah as if they were looking for something that would mark them as different, like a set of gills or a hidden tail. But they were good at making themselves invisible.

Ada was impressed by how fast they were learning. On Sundays, they watched *Bugs Bunny* and *Tom and Jerry* cartoons, which were full of classical music. Norah sat with her cardboard piano across her knees and pretended to play the notes. She figured out that she could learn how to play a song by listening to it and played each one over and over until she got it right.

───

Laurel started booking appointments with real estate agents to look at houses. Sometimes the house was an hour or so away, so they woke early and piled into the Nissan in their pajamas, still half asleep. The warmth of the sun climbed into the car with them like a fifth passenger. In the back seat, Norah and Ingrid changed into their clothes. They wriggled out of their pajamas and into shorts and T-shirts. Elena turned the radio on, and everyone sang along.

The houses they looked at were large, historic, and way out of their price range. Laurel and Elena knew they couldn't afford to live in any of them, but all it took to convince the real estate agents they were in the market was to wear expensive-looking pantsuits and large sunglasses. No one had to know that the clothes came from the thrift store. When Laurel and Elena dressed like that, Ingrid thought they looked like movie stars.

After a couple of years of doing this, one summer day they drove to see a historic inn on the water. It was the biggest property they had ever visited. In the car on the way there, Norah and Ingrid ate raw potatoes like they were apples. The gritty, chalky taste was like eating the earth. But they were only allowed one small potato each, because in large quantities they were poisonous.

Arabella by the Sea had three floors, twenty-five guest rooms, and five cottages scattered in the woods along the edge of the property. The place had its own pond, complete with ducks and wooden rowboats. Laurel had shown the girls pictures online the day before, on the computer in Ada's office. But when they walked into the lobby, with its huge stone fireplace and wood-panelled walls, the girls stopped and stared. Everything looked so much bigger than in the pictures. There was a grand wooden staircase which split in two like in a mansion in the movies. Ingrid looked down at her dirty sneakers against the floral carpet runner and wanted desperately to belong there.

Elena and Laurel followed the real estate agent into the dining room as she told them the history of the place. Joyce, the agent, was wearing white jeans, a white T-shirt, and a bright yellow blazer. She had on white, high-heeled sandals which had sunk into the grass outside the inn and now had clumps of dirt and grass stuck on the pointy heels. She was also wearing a pearl necklace, and each pearl gleamed like a bead of water.

Arabella by the Sea had closed down at the end of the last

tourist season because the owners had moved back to Ontario. They had hoped to sell it before summer, but it was nearly the end of August, and the place was still on the market. The owners were very open to offers. Joyce told Laurel and Elena all of this as they stood in the dining room. The air smelled stale, like the windows hadn't been opened in a long time. There were white sheets over all the furniture, and Norah noticed the shape of a baby grand piano in the corner. Ingrid took her sister's hand and they slipped out of the room. They followed the floral carpet runner up the wide staircase to the second floor to explore on their own.

Every door along the hallway was locked, but they tried the knobs anyway. The wood panelling reminded Ingrid of a church. They climbed the stairs to the third floor, which was smaller and had only a few rooms. Ingrid went straight to the one at the top of the stairs and when she tried the doorknob it swung open. She stood in front of the doorway for a moment before she stepped inside.

The biggest bed she had ever seen was placed with a view of the window, through which the ocean was visible. A pristine white duvet and half a dozen oversize pillows covered the bed. Soft green carpet, two wingback chairs, and a small antique desk completed the room. The walls were wood panelled, like the rest of the inn, which gave the room a cozy library feel. Ingrid stepped over to the window and Norah hovered in the doorway, glancing down the stairs. Up close, Ingrid realized the window was actually a door that led out onto a small balcony overlooking the sea. She unlatched it and stepped out into the salty air. Steep wooden stairs led down from the balcony to the ground. Ingrid leaned against the railing and breathed deeply. The smell of Prince Edward Island in the summer was her favourite smell in the world. Earthy clay, sharp seaweed, and the hint of salt on the breeze. She looked back into the room where Norah stood running her hand over the soft white bedspread like it was a cat.

On their way back downstairs, Ingrid was very tempted to slide down the curved wooden banister, but Norah said no. Elena and Laurel were sitting on the sofas by the fireplace in the lobby, posed rigidly on the white sheet covers. Joyce stood in front of them like she was giving a presentation, talking about how the current owners had kept a fire roaring all the time, even in August. Norah and Ingrid wandered past them back into the dining room, which reminded them of the inside of a ship, with its wooden ceiling, curved walls, and creaking wooden floor. Ingrid wanted them to be able to buy Arabella by the Sea more than any other place they'd visited. She pictured herself singing for the guests in the evening while they ate lobster dipped in butter.

Norah stood next to the piano. She lifted a corner of the dusty white sheet and gasped when she saw the black lacquer. It was the nicest piano she had ever seen. She touched the top of the fallboard with one tentative finger.

Play it, Ingrid said.

I can't, Norah said. I don't know how.

Yes you do, silly. The keys are the same.

With trembling hands, Norah pulled part of the sheet away so she could lift the fallboard to reveal the keys. She sat on the bench, which was also covered by a white sheet, and breathed in. Closing her eyes, she breathed out and started to play.

The first few notes of *"Für Elise"* drifted into the stale air, and there was a scuffle of feet as Joyce, Laurel, and Elena appeared in the dining room. Laurel opened her mouth to say something, but Elena grabbed her arm and Laurel was silent. Ingrid stood next to the piano while Norah played, and when the piece was finished, there was a heavy moment of silence before Joyce started to clap.

Norah flinched but didn't turn around.

Beautiful! Joyce said. Play something else!

Norah turned her head and looked at Ingrid, who noticed her sister's hands were trembling on the keys.

"Stay Awake," Ingrid said under her breath, and Norah nodded once, sat up straighter, and started playing again. Ingrid sang—she sang softer than usual, since the song was a lullaby, and let her voice float to the ceiling. Joyce listened with one hand resting on her clavicle, as if she had never heard children sing or play the piano before. At the end of the song, the three adults clapped and Ingrid did a silly bow as Norah carefully replaced the fallboard and dust sheet, transforming the gleaming black piano back into a ghost.

Do you girls play anywhere? Joyce said. I'd love to bring my friends to see you.

Norah doesn't like playing in front of people, Ingrid said.

Oh, that's too bad, Joyce said. She plays so well.

Norah was still sitting on the piano bench, her shoulders stiff. Ingrid nudged her sister and she stood up, removing herself from the music. She went somewhere different when she played; her entire body relaxed into the keys. Stepping back into the real world from that place seemed painful and awkward for her, as if she were two different people trying to inhabit the same skin.

———

They stopped at a roadside restaurant to eat and fill the car with gas. The four of them sat in a booth by the window and flipped through the menus. The girls' legs stuck to the red vinyl seats and made suction noises when they moved. Ingrid ordered the all-day breakfast with orange juice, while Norah got an egg salad sandwich with fries and chocolate milk.

Maybe you girls should get an act on the go, Elena said before the food arrived. You could play at local pubs and churches, that sort of thing. Everyone would love you!

I don't know about that, Laurel said.

Of course they'd love them! Elena said. Look at them!

That's not what I meant.

Norah drank her chocolate milk from a bendy straw and stared out the window. People filled their cars with gas, bought bags of ice from the large cooler outside the store, and put air in their tires. The window was tinted and made everything look as if it was happening underwater.

I'll do it, Norah said.

Laurel and Elena stopped talking. Ingrid stared at her sister, but Norah continued to stare out the window.

What? Laurel said.

I'll play for people, Norah said. I'll do it as long as Ingrid is the only one who sings.

The server appeared, balancing all four plates, which she expertly set on the table. Her appearance halted the conversation and Laurel picked up her cutlery and unrolled it from the paper napkin. Ingrid took a sip of orange juice and felt the crust of it on her upper lip. She rubbed it away with the back of her hand.

—————

Ingrid and Norah's lives as semi-official musicians began slowly. They told Ada about their plan and she was skeptical, worried about Ingrid overworking her voice. She still didn't have full control of her breath and liked to sing very loudly, which frustrated Ada. But after a few days of thinking, Ada warmed to the idea and helped the girls prepare their first set. It consisted of six songs, all from musicals, simple at the beginning, with crowd favourites at the end. Norah wanted another set, to revolve around a different theme, so they came up with a country set too. Which one they sang would depend on the venue.

With Ada's help, Ingrid tried to strengthen her head voice. But her voice was naturally stronger when she sang from her chest, and Ingrid found it difficult to hit the same notes when she went into her head voice. She was becoming more determined and disciplined, and practised almost as much as Norah.

It was Ada who secured their first gig, at the church where Laurel tended the cemetery. Ada attended the Sunday service there and had recently started playing the small organ and some-times the piano. On occasion, she sang with the choir, but only if one of the members was unavailable. During the girls' lessons, Ada told them how she used to teach music at the school, but when her parents died and left her the Blue Moth Motel in their will, she had decided to quit her job to run the place.

There was another teacher there who I knew very well, Ada said. So she took over teaching music.

On the Sunday of their first official performance, Norah and Ingrid wore matching blue plaid dresses whose hemlines hit a bit higher on their legs than they had the previous year. Soon they would be starting Grade Five and Ingrid hoped they could get some new clothes. They didn't own any fancy shoes, so they wore their sneakers and had tried to wipe the red mud off them before they left the Blue Moth, but it hadn't worked. Laurel and Elena came to watch and sat together in the first pew, shoulders touching. Weak light trickled in through the single stained glass window behind the altar and created a rainbow on the floor. The air was musty and smelled like candles and wood. Everything echoed and the silence had a weight.

Ada sat at the organ and played everyone to their seats. The organ was dramatic and deep, like an instrument being played from under the sea. Norah and Ingrid dashed out of the bathroom and stood to the left of the stage with the choir members. Ingrid had expected them to be wearing long flowing robes, but they were in their regular clothes, the men in dress slacks and sports jackets, the women in pastel sweater sets and polyester skirts. In hushed voices, they asked the girls about school and what songs they were going to sing. Ingrid answered everything while Norah stared at her sneakers, the songbook clutched against her chest.

The minister said a few words to begin the service and then the girls stepped onto the stage. Ingrid would sing "Stay Awake" and "9 to 5," accompanied by Norah. They didn't know any religious songs, but Ada said it was okay. Then Norah would play one of her favourite pieces by Clara Schumann. The minister, Ingrid was pleased to see, was wearing a robe. She had frizzy blond hair and round glasses that made her look like a scientist. But Ingrid liked her soft voice and cheerful manner. With a sweep of her arm, she introduced the girls, and Norah took her place at the piano. She arranged her songbook and Ingrid took her spot by the microphone. The entire congregation was very quiet, as if they were holding their breath. Ingrid looked out at Laurel and Elena, who gave a thumbs-up. When Norah was ready, she made eye contact with Ingrid and they began.

It was the first time Ingrid had sung into a microphone. The sound of her voice projected to the back of the small church felt like an electric shock. It almost didn't sound like her voice. Norah played precisely, her eyes fixed on her songbook. The performance wasn't as perfect as the one at Arabella by the Sea, but everyone applauded when they finished, and Ingrid took a bow. Norah rustled the pages of music to find the next song as Ada, Laurel, and Elena clapped the loudest. Norah knew the music by heart but still liked to have it with her. It gave her something physical to look at.

The second song went over even better than the first. It was more upbeat, and some people clapped along. The congregation seemed to get a kick out of hearing two young girls sing about the difficulties of a nine-to-five job. Ingrid watched Ada's face for a reaction and saw she was smiling, her face a bit paler than usual. When the song was over, Ingrid did another bow and everyone clapped again. Then she sat down on the piano bench next to Norah, who flipped to another page in the songbook and breathed in. When she exhaled, she began to play. Everyone was silent, motionless. No squeaking pews, no muffled sneezes, no shuffling feet. Norah held everyone within the music, and it was a place they wanted to stay.

After the performance, the girls sat through the church service, their first ever. Ingrid sang along with all the hymns, following the words in the leather-bound book with its tissue-paper pages. She found that she stood up straighter and sang better when she was surrounded by the rest of the congregation. The choir, standing behind the minister, swayed slightly to the music and some of them didn't look down at their hymn books at all. Ada played the piano. Ingrid thought she seemed like a different person away from the Blue Moth, behind the church piano: younger, and less strict.

In the church basement after the service, everyone ate cucumber sandwiches cut into triangles and drank apple juice out of paper cups. Ingrid had never eaten a cucumber sandwich before, but she liked how it tasted like the garden. Many people came up to the girls and complimented their music and asked if they would be there every week. Ingrid glanced around the room for Ada and saw her standing next to a large stainless steel urn dispensing coffee into mugs. Laurel and Elena had disappeared, and Norah was getting overwhelmed, so in a break between conversations, Ingrid wrapped a couple of sandwiches in a paper napkin and took her sister's hand. They ran back up the stairs to the nave, their steps echoing as they dashed down the aisle and out into the sunshine.

Norah stopped and breathed deeply when they reached the cemetery, then they continued through the grass and down the path to the beach. They sat on the surfboard tree and ate the sandwiches, which tasted even better in the salty air. The tide was out, revealing hidden sandbars, and the sand was rippled from the water moving away. Pools collected in the troughs of the ripples and sparkled in the sun. A few squawking seagulls bobbed in the bigger pools.

Look, Norah said. She pointed down the beach where smoke was rising from a barrel propped up in the sand. Three women in hooded black cloaks stood around the fire and a group of people in regular clothes were gathered a few feet away from them, watching. The girls jumped down from the tree and went to get a closer look.

As they neared the gathering, Ingrid realized the women were speaking but she couldn't understand what they were saying. The words were English, but when strung together they didn't make much sense. Up close, Ingrid saw that the fire was in an old washing machine drum. The smell of smoke wafted into the air and made Ingrid hungry for marshmallows. A breeze pushed back the hood of one woman's cloak and revealed curly bright red hair. The witches circled the fire, their words like a song Ingrid wanted to understand. As they spoke, they produced items from inside their cloaks and dropped them into the metal drum.

After a few minutes, the witches moved away and disappeared into the woods. The people in regular clothes followed them, but Norah and Ingrid stayed behind on the beach. Ingrid went to take a closer look at the fire. The flames were regular flames and there was no trace of the items the witches had dropped inside. Two men came walking towards them, each with heavy-looking buckets in their hands, calling out for the girls to go away. They started to, but they stopped and looked behind them. One man had his back turned now, as he poured water over the fire. The other man was holding a clipboard.

Norah grabbed Ingrid's hand and they ran back along the beach and up the path to the church. By the time they reached the cemetery again, the congregation had dispersed and only Ada remained, waiting for the girls on a bench by the church door. When Ada had sat at the organ, her posture was perfect. On the bench she looked slumped and older again. But when she saw the girls running between the headstones, she stood and stretched out her arms.

CHAPTER 9

Lewes

I've quit my job at the pub.

Even though it isn't the type of job I want to do forever, I liked the atmosphere and enjoyed talking to different people every evening. It's easy to forget about the world when you're focused on balancing trays of frothy beer and fish and chips. The floor was sticky no matter how well it was mopped the night before and my sneakers stuck with each step, like walking in mud. There was a large stone hearth where a fire was always roaring, no matter the season, and the ceiling was low, with heavy wooden beams. Before I moved to the UK, I thought Prince Edward Island had old buildings. But there are people here who live in cottages built in the 1600s.

A couple of weeks after my doctor's appointment, I sit at the kitchen table doing math. I moved to the UK three years ago without fully considering the cost of living, and now I'm in trouble. With my three jobs—waiting tables, cleaning, and singing at the pub—I manage to scrape by. Susan is kind and doesn't charge as much as she could for the room. But when I take two jobs out of the equation, there's no way to make the math work. I have some tips saved from the pub gigs, but within two months I'll be broke. I know if I ask to move in with Julia, she'll let me, but I don't want to ask. Staying over at her place occasionally is completely different from living there. I know she would welcome me in, push her clothes over in the closet and clear out a drawer or two to make room, but it's her world, not mine.

I haven't told anyone back home about my voice. When Norah tried to video chat, I texted her back and said the Wi-Fi was down and I wouldn't be able to go on video for a few weeks at the earliest. The only people who know are Susan, Julia, and my voice teacher, Isla. I sent her a text a couple of days after the appointment to explain why I wouldn't be at my lessons for a while. She texted back a lovely message and told me to reach out if I needed anything. Even though it's warm for April, I keep a scarf wrapped around my neck. I don't know if this is helpful for my vocal cords, but it makes me feel better.

Julia buys me a silky turquoise scarf the colour of pool water and I wear it every day. It also reminds me of Ada, who would know exactly what to do if only I could ask her.

CHAPTER 10

Prince Edward Island, 2002 to 2003

After their first performance, Ingrid became obsessed with singing. She had loved it before, but when she heard her voice projected through the microphone, something changed. It was about power; when she was on stage, she was in charge. Everyone had to listen, wanted to listen, and Ingrid wanted to sing her best for them. It wasn't until much later that Ingrid realized there are people who don't like it when girls raise their voices.

She and Norah kept up their lessons with Ada, who decided they should only perform pieces composed by women. Ada stood next to the piano with one hand on her hip and the other resting on the fallboard. This day, she was wearing a necklace made of shells that Norah had given her. The girls hoped that by giving Ada presents, they would let her know they loved her.

Ada let the girls stop practising early because of the heat. Even though it was September, the air was still heavy and the ceiling fan in the breakfast room only pushed it around. A guest had left a paperback behind on a table, its pages now warped and bloated with moisture. Norah and Ingrid ran out and jumped into the pool, still wearing their clothes. When Ingrid surfaced, beads of water dripping from her eyelashes, she saw Ada running after them with her dress billowing out. With a whoop, she jumped into the pool and surfaced, sending a spray of water towards the girls with the back of her hand.

That year, Ada started biweekly bingo games in the breakfast room. Every Monday and Friday night, the room was transformed into a bingo hall. Norah and Ingrid helped clean off the tables and sweep the floor. Ada bought a bingo machine where the balls rolled around inside a cage. Ingrid would spin the cage really fast so the balls became a multicoloured blur. The players brought their own daubers. Only guests from the Blue Moth showed up to play the first night, but by the third week word had got out and people showed up from all over.

By December, Ada had to turn people away because there weren't enough seats. Norah and Ingrid sat inside the door on plastic lawn chairs to keep count of the players. The women had canvas bags to carry their rainbow bingo daubers and chocolate bars. Ada put Norah and Ingrid in charge of crowd control and of pointing the way to the bathroom. The girls snuck Styrofoam cups of juice, and when her cup was empty Ingrid chewed around the rim and spit pieces of Styrofoam back in.

The Blue Moth was still struggling to fill its rooms and Ada often worked long into the night. A patterned sofa appeared in the office and Ada slept there when she worked late. She wrote advertisements for newspapers and researched the other hotels in the area to find out what they offered their guests. One evening after Christmas, Ingrid woke up alone in the bed. She sat up and looked out the window at the courtyard and noticed the light on in the office. Ingrid shimmied quietly out of bed, wrapped a blanket around her shoulders, and crossed the courtyard to investigate. There was a layer of fresh squeaky snow, her footprints the first to break its pristine surface.

Ada was sitting behind the desk at her computer and Norah was on the sofa, wrapped in blankets, reading Ingrid's copy of *Little Women*. Neither of them noticed Ingrid looking in the window and she felt as if she were watching a scene from a movie. The window was streaked with grime, which softened everything inside. They looked so content sitting there that Ingrid didn't want to ruin the moment by barging in. But she was jealous. Ada said she didn't play favourites, but Ingrid knew Ada thought Norah was more talented. Ada would never say so, but Ingrid saw the way her grandmother looked at Norah when she played, how Ada's eyes brightened and she looked younger for a moment. Ingrid watched them for a few more minutes before she crossed the courtyard again. Her footsteps were still visible in the snow and she followed them, scuffing her feet to disguise the tracks.

Norah and Ingrid's second performance had been at a small pub in the city on a Sunday afternoon. The girls tried to dress in a way that made them appear more grown-up. Ingrid settled on a long-sleeved, tie-dyed shirt tucked into jeans. Norah chose a white blouse and long blue skirt.

The five of them piled into the Nissan. Ada sat up front with Laurel, who turned the radio to the country station. She rolled the windows down even though the air was chilly. Elena put her arm out the window and Ingrid did the same on the other side.

At the pub, they found a table close to the front and sat down. Norah sized up the piano, which was an upright with a layer of dust on the top. There wasn't a stage, just the piano and microphone set up in the corner. Faint country music played over the speakers and there was a gentle hum of conversation, but the place wasn't busy. It smelled of yeasty beer and fried food. Laurel urged the girls to go introduce themselves to the pub owner, a wiry, stern-looking woman with black hair who was pouring a pint into a tilted glass.

The woman glanced up as they approached, and smiled, which changed her face. She transformed from a no-nonsense pub owner to a schoolteacher impressed by her students. She slid the pint down the wooden bar towards a man in a plaid shirt and he lifted his hand to stop its motion. She wiped her hands on her black apron.

You must be Norah and Ingrid, she said. I'm Jane. Welcome to The Stone Hearth. Now, which is which?

Ingrid introduced herself and Norah. They shook Jane's hand and she gave them each a plastic cup filled with Coke from the soda fountain. Bubbles stuck to the plastic and rose to the top. Ingrid took a sip and the fizz tickled her nose and made her eyes water. Jane went to Norah and Ingrid's table to meet everyone and explained that performers ate for free after their set. It was as if the girls were being initiated into a secret club they hadn't known existed. Their set wasn't due to start for another half-hour, so they waited and drank their pop. Ada told Ingrid that pop, alcohol and cigarettes were bad for her voice, but that pop was okay in moderation.

A few more people had arrived and filled some of the tables. As Ingrid approached the microphone, she adjusted her shirt. The people in the pub might keep talking and drinking. It was a different crowd from the churchgoers, who were required to listen quietly. The girls would have to win the attention of the pub audience and prove they were worth listening to. Norah slid onto the piano bench and opened her songbook. They were going to perform their country set. Jane lowered the microphone and tapped on the mouthpiece a few times.

Now listen up! she said. Our performers this afternoon are sisters Ingrid and Norah. They're going to sing some country hits for you. Enjoy!

She stepped away and motioned for Ingrid to take her place. Ingrid cleared her throat and stepped forward. At the table, Ada nodded at the girls in encouragement. Ingrid turned towards Norah, and they began.

At first, Ingrid's voice was quiet and uncertain, but it strengthened as she moved through the set. Norah's playing was perfect, and when Ingrid faltered, Norah played a bit louder to cover up the mistakes. Everyone clapped after each song and only talked quietly throughout. By the time the set ended, all the tables were full and there was a cluster of people standing along the bar and inside the front door. Ingrid's face was flushed as she finished the final song and looked around at all the faces turned in her direction.

Norah stood beside her and they bowed. They headed back to their table and Ada stood up to embrace them. Jane reappeared at the table with two more cups of Coke and said she wanted the girls to perform every Sunday.

Everyone loved you, she said as she set the fresh pop on the table with an envelope and stacked the empty cups and plates onto a tray. The envelope said "Norah and Ingrid." Just like that, the girls had their first consistent paying gig.

Keep that safe, Laurel said, and Norah took the envelope and folded it into the pocket of her skirt.

Ingrid ordered a basket of french fries and Norah ordered a plate of nachos. The food arrived and Ingrid got grease and ketchup all over her fingers. If playing gigs meant eating out for free and being allowed to drink fizzy pop, Ingrid was on board. The added incentive of having a bit of money of their own was exciting. Laurel had given them each a Mason jar with their name on it to keep their earnings safe. She had explained the benefits of saving money for a rainy day and kept her own Mason jar under her bed for emergencies.

On the drive home, Ingrid had the hiccups from the Coke. She looked out the car window and saw a man with a guitar standing under an awning outside a bookshop. He was singing a country song and his voice echoed down the street. She nudged Norah with her foot and pointed as they drove by.

Let's do that, Ingrid said. But Norah shook her head.

Ingrid watched the man until they turned the corner and he disappeared from view. She slumped against the car door and felt the sugar from the pop coursing through her body. It made her hands shake and all she wanted was to be at a microphone again.

The girls saved their money from the pub gigs in their Mason jars and tucked them under their bed. They kept a few dollars every week for pocket money and went shopping at the thrift store. Norah was obsessed with china teacups and saucers with floral patterns, and with books. Ingrid kept a row of Nancy Drew novels in the drawer of their bedside table, yellow spines facing up. Norah also bought sheet music and taught herself to play the pieces. Even when their lesson with Ada was over, Norah would stay in the breakfast room and listen to CDs, while Ingrid ran off to feed the seagulls or deliver towels or help Elena clean the rooms. She sang as she worked, so it was kind of like practising.

Ingrid's favourite chore to help with was changing the sheets on the beds. Elena would make up stories about the guests based on what she saw in their rooms.

I'm very curious about how people live, Elena said. I trust the people who have books in their rooms and I wonder about the ones who bring five pairs of shoes for a beach vacation.

Ingrid helped Elena pull the fitted sheets over the mattress and smooth them. If there was a nice breeze and the air didn't smell like the sewage lagoon, they opened all the windows and let the rooms air out. When they reached their room, which they did last, Ingrid kicked off her shoes and lay down like a starfish in the middle of her and Norah's bed. With a snap of white cotton, Elena unfurled the top sheet so it floated down on top of Ingrid, who watched as it fell. It felt like slipping beneath the surface of the pool, cool and refreshing. The sheet created a gentle whoosh and dust sparkled in the air.

In the spring, a woman named Paula from the congregation died and Ada asked if the girls would perform at the funeral. Ada wanted Norah to sing with Ingrid while Ada played the piano, and Norah agreed. As Paula had requested, everyone wore bright colours and the girls weren't allowed to sing anything sad. As Ingrid walked through the cemetery towards the church, the birds singing in the trees and the smell of the earth waking up filled her with energy. It seemed wrong for a person to leave the world in the spring, when everything was coming alive again.

Dressed in bright florals, Norah, Ada, and Ingrid took to the stage. The closed casket was surrounded by a rainbow of peonies and zinnias. Holding hands, Norah and Ingrid sang "Dancing Queen" by ABBA, which had been Paula's favourite song. Everyone clapped along and seemed happy, but it was a heavy happiness. Ingrid tried to ignore the casket at the base of the stage because the idea of being stuck inside it made her feel claustrophobic. Norah held Ingrid's hand so tightly the bones of her fingers squeezed together, but Norah sang bravely, her voice only a bit softer than Ingrid's.

When the song was finished, the girls returned to their seats next to Laurel and Elena and listened to a few stories from Paula's friends. Then the pallbearers lifted the casket and carried it down the aisle. Everyone followed along behind, filing out into the cemetery. Norah took Ada's hand and they walked in front of Ingrid. At the doorway, Ada leaned down and whispered something in Norah's ear; she let go of Ada and turned to reach for Ingrid's hand. And then the girls were running, away from the casket and the congregation, towards the path to the beach. They kicked off their shoes and ran barefoot across the sand, which was still cold from winter. The wind blew in from the water and their dresses flapped as they ran towards the waves.

The water made their legs go numb but they splashed and ran through the waves, making footprints in the sand that were erased almost immediately. There was a wooden lobster trap half-submerged on the beach and they took turns jumping over it to see who could leap the highest. Ingrid and Norah were the only people there, and Norah started singing. She sang louder than she ever had before, and her voice soared over the waves. As she ran along the shoreline, her voice jumped every time her feet hit the sand.

The girls heard Ada call, and they turned and saw that she had followed them to the beach. They started running towards her, their hair streaming out behind them, their voices uneven and distorted by the wind. Norah leaped into the air so high it looked as if she were trying to fly away from her sister while Ingrid clutched her hand, trying to keep her on the ground.

CHAPTER 11

Lewes

Julia has a membership at the local leisure centre and she lets me borrow her card so I can use the indoor pool. I'd rather do outdoor swimming if possible, but I need something to distract myself. I enjoy the repetition of going back and forth along the lane.

In the change room, I put on my suit and leave my bag in a locker. I tuck my towel under my arm and step out onto the pool deck, my flip-flops slapping in the puddles. No matter the season, the warm, humid climate at an indoor pool is consistent. I understand how some people might find the consistency reassuring, but I prefer the unexpectedness of the ocean and even the sliminess of ponds.

I choose a lane and leave my towel on a nearby bench. There are two large pools—one for lane swimming and the other for kids. The kids' pool has a waterslide that Norah and I would've loved when we were young. Goggles in place, I step up on the block and dive in.

Underwater, every sound becomes muffled and soft. The voices of the people on the pool deck disappear and I'm alone in watery silence. It's the only type of quiet I enjoy, maybe because it's more of a hum than a silence. I swim underwater for as long as I can hold my breath, staring down at the blue tiles. Surfacing is jarring; voices echo off the walls and sound louder than they actually are. When I reach the other end of the lane, I catch my breath and dive under again.

This time, I swim all the way to the bottom of the pool. My ears crack as they adjust to the pressure and my lungs begin to ache for air. As I push off from the bottom, I wonder if swimming has the potential to become my new form of singing. I could become a lifeguard, wear a red bathing suit, and sit on one of those chairs high above the pool. It would be a very different life, but one I could enjoy. If I trained to be a lifeguard, I could join a rescue crew back on Prince Edward Island and spend my summers patrolling the beaches and the colder months lifeguarding at indoor pools.

I surface and begin an easy breaststroke along the lane. The rhythmic breathing calms my mind and soon I block out the noise around me. I pretend I'm back in the pool at the Blue Moth, swimming at night with Norah. She challenged me to races and breath-holding competitions even though I always won. Her determination kept her going; she wasn't discouraged by losing.

At the end of the lane, I prop my arms up on the wall under the block to take a break. In the next lane, I notice my singing teacher, Isla, doing laps. I wave when she reaches the end of the pool and she lifts her goggles to the top of her head.

Ingrid! I've never seen you here before, Isla says. She treads water, her black swimming cap and matching black swimsuit look much more professional than my mismatched outfit. Do you swim here often?

I shake my head.

Well, it's good to see you, she says. I hope to see you back at my studio very soon. And if you need anything, don't hesitate to call.

I nod in what I hope is a grateful way and she pushes off from the wall to do another lap. I pull myself out of the pool, my energy gone. I put my flip-flops back on and return to the change room to stand under the warm shower, letting the roar of it fill my ears until it sounds like I'm underwater again.

CHAPTER 12

Prince Edward Island, 2003

A few weeks after the funeral, the girls were hired to perform at a wedding in one of the city parks. The bride, Alice, was the daughter of one of Ada's friends and she wore a pale pink dress instead of white. She made flower crowns for the girls to wear and placed them on their heads herself, complimenting Norah on her golden hair.

It was a small wedding of close friends and family. The groom was short and pale, and he swayed slowly back and forth as he stood in the park's gazebo next to the minister. Ingrid thought Alice was much too pretty for him. Alice cried quietly as her dad led her up the short aisle, their arms linked at the elbow.

Norah and Ingrid sat next to Ada on white plastic chairs set up in rows in the gazebo. Ada was wearing one of her long floral dresses with flat sandals and a scarf tied in a band over her curly grey hair. There was an upright piano, and a man in a suit played the wedding march. Alice clutched a bouquet of roses and baby's breath with both hands.

The sky was blue and cloudless. Ingrid could smell the sea. It was the first wedding they had been to, and she liked it a lot more than the funeral. But it was similar in the way people gathered to say goodbye as a person moved on to another life. Ingrid still believed people went somewhere when they died, thanks to Ada's explanation of heaven. But she wasn't sure what that place looked like, so in her mind marriage wasn't much different. The bride was leaving one life to begin another, and Ingrid wasn't sure which life was better. Maybe Alice didn't know either.

Norah held Ada's hand during the ceremony and Ingrid tried to understand what the vows meant. Afterwards, the bride and groom left in a horse-drawn carriage. Before they pulled away, the bride tossed her bouquet over her shoulder and Ada caught it out of reflex to prevent it from hitting Norah on the head. Everyone clapped and Ada held the bouquet in the air, looking a bit embarrassed. She handed it to Norah, who held it against her chest, smelling the flowers with her eyes closed.

The carriage left for a short drive around the city and the guests made their way to the reception venue. The clip-clop of the horses' hooves against the pavement echoed along the narrow street, and drivers honked their horns and yelled congratulations out their windows. The Clydesdales were huge, with long, feathery white hair on their lower legs, dinner plate–sized hooves, and their long manes were braided with pink ribbons. When they arrived outside the venue, Norah and Ingrid went over to pet them. They smelled warm and earthy. Ingrid ripped up a handful of grass and fed it to one of them and he gently lipped the strands out of her hand.

The historical carriage house had creaky wooden floors and smelled like horses and roses. There was a baby grand in the corner and the man from the ceremony played a classical piece as the guests found their seats at the tables which were set up around the room. At the front, a long table was set for the wedding party and on a smaller table next to it sat the cake, three tiers of white icing and pale pink icing roses. When the man finished playing and stood up, Ingrid and Norah made their way to him and introduced themselves. He gathered up his music and Norah took his place on the bench.

It was the most impressive piano Norah had ever had the opportunity to play, even better than the one at Arabella by the Sea. She ran her fingers softly over the keys, as if she were talking to the piano, asking if she was allowed to play it. In the centre of the room, Alice leaned against the groom, who had his arm tucked around her waist. The song she had requested for their first dance was "At Last," by Etta James. Ingrid had been practising to make sure she hit every note just right. It was a difficult song and she wanted to do it justice. Norah began to play.

The bride and groom swayed in a golden spotlight, and when the song was over they motioned for everyone to join them. Norah played a few instrumental pieces before the father–daughter dance, for which Ingrid joined in and sang "I Will Always Love You." Her rendition was true to Dolly Parton's original version. As Ingrid sang, she watched Alice dance with her father. What did it mean to promise to spend the rest of your life with someone, no matter what? It seemed like such a big promise to make, such a long period of time, that Ingrid couldn't fathom it. She wondered if Laurel and Elena wanted to get married, even though they weren't officially allowed.

Norah played a few more classical pieces and some upbeat numbers, which everyone enjoyed. They cut the cake and the groom smeared icing on the bride's nose. Ingrid looked for Laurel and Elena in the crowd and saw them dancing together, like they were in a movie. Laurel moved gracefully and Ingrid hoped she would be as beautiful as her mom someday. Under the golden light, Elena's red hair glowed and she pulled Laurel close.

<hr>

At the end of summer, the four of them went on a vacation to Nova Scotia. It was the first family trip they had ever taken, and the four-hour drive was the longest time they had ever spent in a car. Norah and Ingrid sat in the back seat eating blueberries out of a green cardboard box. Laurel had bought these for them at a roadside stand. Laurel drove and Elena navigated using a tattered paper map from the glove compartment. Ingrid sang along to the country music station in an exaggerated twang until Norah told her to stop. So Ingrid started doing vocal warm-up exercises instead, humming and buzzing her lips together.

Ingrid, that's enough, Laurel said.

Ingrid stuck out her tongue, which was stained blue from the berries. Norah rolled her eyes.

Ingrid tipped her head back and looked out the rear window to see what the world looked like upside down. Treetops flashed by so fast they looked like birds, with clouds shaped like horses, dragons, and music notes. Norah was practising with her cardboard piano keys propped on her knees. Ingrid wondered what the music sounded like inside her head. She decided that everyone essentially lived in two worlds—the real one and the one within their head—and no matter how well you knew a person, it was impossible to access both of them. Everyone got to keep a little part of themselves secret, and maybe that was for the best. In the front seat, Elena took a plastic bag of watermelon slices out of the cooler at her feet and handed it back to the girls. They ate eagerly, juice sliding down their chins, and spit the watermelon seeds at each other.

As they drove across the Confederation Bridge, Ingrid pushed herself up in her seat in an attempt to see over the concrete barricades, but the car was too low and she only caught a glimpse of the sparkling ocean. Behind them, the sandstone cliffs of Prince Edward Island slowly disappeared. As they entered New Brunswick, the highway was lined with pine trees; Norah hoped they might see a bear. The girls started counting transport trucks, but they soon fell asleep and didn't wake up until they arrived at Blomidon Provincial Park.

When they found the campsite, Laurel and Elena unloaded the car while Ingrid and Norah ran down to explore the beach. A set of steep wooden stairs led down the cliff to the sand and Norah held the railing tightly as she descended. The sand and rocks were dark red sandstone, similar in colour to some of the beaches at home, but the water was tinged brown along the shore. When Ingrid waded in, her legs disappeared. Mud squished between her toes. She realized the tide was going out—the water receded from her legs. Laurel had told them not to swim unsupervised because the tides were stronger here, and now Ingrid understood what she meant. Within a few minutes, her feet were visible again. The girls squelched through the muddy sand towards a waterfall cascading down the cliffside. After four hours in the car, the cold water woke them up. They let it drench their clothes and hair, shaking their heads so the water flew. Goosebumps rose on Ingrid's arms and legs as water trickled down her back.

The sky was blue when they left Prince Edward Island but had since clouded over. When Ingrid stepped out of the waterfall, a few drops of rain landed on her arms. Norah, standing a few feet away, turned her palms up to the sky. Over the ocean, dark clouds were rolling in and the girls raced back up the stairs to the campsite.

With the tent secured, Elena had lit a fire and was boiling water in a stainless steel kettle she had rigged up to hang on a stick above the flames. Laurel sat cross-legged in the doorway of the tent, reading. Ingrid dove into the tent and snuggled her face into the pillows, despite Laurel's protests about wet hair. The rain held off just long enough that the fire didn't go out. Then, as she lay in the tent, Ingrid listened to the sound of rain against the fabric and started to drift off. It seemed like it was coming down much harder than it was, the raindrops amplified by the tent.

The tent was spacious enough for the four of them to sleep cozily and have enough room to sit up. Norah could almost stand up completely, but Ingrid had to stoop. She had grown taller than her older sister in the past few months. They played Crazy Eights, Go Fish, and Gin Rummy. Whoever won the hand got to choose the next game. The sound of the rain intensified and cooking supper over the fire became impossible, so they ate jam sandwiches and crackers.

Before bed, the girls ran through the rain to the washrooms to brush their teeth. The grass felt slimy against their bare feet. Ants, fleeing their water-soaked tunnels, marched into the washrooms in orderly lines and crawled up the walls. While Norah brushed her teeth, Ingrid watched the ants march up the door frame in a perfect line. She wondered what ants thought about, and if they thought at all, or just existed.

The morning was foggy and calm, mist hanging over the water like a grey blanket, making everything soft around the edges. Elena cooked oatmeal in a pot and Laurel boiled water for coffee on a campstove on the picnic table. Everything took longer to make than when they were home, so Ingrid pulled a hoodie on over her pajamas and decided to climb one of the nearby pine trees. The sap smelled delicious, almost good enough to eat. It made her hands sticky. Halfway up, she draped her legs on either side of a branch and sat there high above the campsite.

There are more dark clouds over the water! she called down.

Probably just the fog, Laurel said. Breakfast is ready now, come down!

A mug of steaming, watery instant coffee sat on the table and Ingrid looked at Laurel before she took a sip.

Don't tell Ada, Laurel said.

The liquid was bitter, so Ingrid put more milk and sugar in. It still had a sharp, metallic tinge from the tin mug, but Norah seemed to be enjoying it, so Ingrid kept drinking hers too.

Morning was always Ingrid's favourite time. She liked to see the day begin. And here, in a new place, anything felt possible. Ingrid ate her oatmeal, sweetened with brown sugar. Overhead, a couple of crows hopped in the branches of the pine tree, waiting to see if they would leave any scraps.

Where would you live, if you could live anywhere in the world? Ingrid asked Laurel.

Italy.

Why?

Because of the vineyards, Laurel said. And the beaches.

Where would you live? Elena asked Ingrid.

I don't know yet, Ingrid said. There are too many places to choose from.

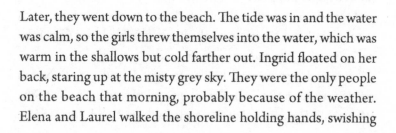

Later, they went down to the beach. The tide was in and the water was calm, so the girls threw themselves into the water, which was warm in the shallows but cold farther out. Ingrid floated on her back, staring up at the misty grey sky. They were the only people on the beach that morning, probably because of the weather. Elena and Laurel walked the shoreline holding hands, swishing their feet through the water. Norah swam for a few minutes then sat at the edge of the water and scooped up handfuls of muddy clay and wiped it over her arms and legs like lotion. When all her bare skin was covered, she stood and waded back into the water to wash it away.

Ingrid floated like a starfish until she heard Laurel's raised voice and looked up. Norah was standing on one foot, like a seabird. She had her other foot raised and the sole of it was splashed with red. Elena scooped Norah up in one swift motion as if she were a child of six rather than twelve. Swimming fast, Ingrid arrived back on shore and ran over to where the three of them were now crouching on the sand, inspecting Norah's foot. She wasn't crying, but her face was pale, lips tinged blue. Elena poured water from a bottle over Norah's foot and wiped away the blood with the edge of Norah's T-shirt. There was a long slice across the arch of her foot.

Probably a razor clam shell, hidden in the mud, Elena said.

She wrapped Norah's foot with the T-shirt, tying it in a tight knot as it continued to bleed, and lifted her into her arms again.

I can hop, Norah said. I'm okay.

But Elena didn't put her down. They climbed the stairs toward the campsite and Ingrid, behind them, watched Norah's feet bob at eye level, the blood soaking through the T-shirt like paint.

Norah received three neat stitches, a pair of crutches, and a knitted finger puppet. It was made of blue yarn and had a cat face and ears sewn on with embroidery thread. It was a toy for a much younger kid, but Norah wore the puppet on her index finger the entire way back to the campsite from the hospital.

It rained for the next four days straight. Ingrid sat with Norah in the tent with the door flap open and played cards or I Spy. When Norah grew tired of those games, Ingrid read aloud to her.

Rain dripped through the pine trees and the air was scented with sap and reminded Ingrid of how the breakfast room smelled at Christmas when they brought in the real tree. The few other families who had been staying at nearby campsites all packed up and left, and they soon had the place to themselves. Norah complained about how the crutches dug into her armpits and refused to use them. She hopped around on one foot or stayed in the tent. When Ingrid went out exploring, Norah practised piano on her cardboard keys or sketched the flowers and plants Elena collected.

When the rain slackened, Ingrid went for walks along the beach. At low tide, she walked towards the water but it took forever to reach it. As she walked, her feet sank deeper and deeper into the red mud and she worried about cutting her foot. When she finally reached the water, she waded out but it stayed the same depth for a very long time. The Bay of Fundy has the highest tides in the world, and as Ingrid watched the water, she could tell whether the tide was coming in or going out just by waiting for a few minutes. She was walking on the ocean floor. Rather than being full of life, it appeared to be a barren stretch of mud. But underneath the surface was where everything was happening.

The final morning at the campsite dawned sunny and warm, a perfect late August day. They ate granola bars for breakfast, not wanting to waste the morning with cooking. Norah's foot was a lot better, but she was still hopping around—Elena gave her a piggyback down to the beach. The tide was going out, so it wasn't safe to swim. Ingrid wrote their names in the sand with the end of a stick and drew a big heart around all of them. She ran in circles, dragging the stick so it made wave patterns in the sand.

As they turned to walk back along the beach, Norah heard something in the brush along the sandstone bank. A small black cat with white-tipped paws emerged, mewing loudly, and wound himself around Elena's legs. The cat was skinny, missing some fur and a piece of one ear. But he was energetic and started purring. Norah slid down from Elena's back and let the cat sniff her hand. He rubbed his face against her fingers and closed his eyes, purring even louder. Norah scooped the cat into her arms.

We're keeping him, she said. He wants to come home with us.

He might belong to someone, Laurel said, even though it was clear from the state of his fur and prominent spine that no one had looked after him in a long time.

Norah set the cat down on the sand. He followed them the entire way along the beach and up the stairs to the campsite. When they got to their tent, the cat looked at Norah, hopped into the Nissan through the open window, and fell asleep in a patch of sun on the seat.

Well, Laurel said. I guess we have a cat now.

Packing up the campsite and loading everything back into the car felt wrong on such a sunny day. As they drove away, Ingrid looked out the window at the water until it disappeared. The cat, whom Norah called Puss, curled up on Norah's lap and slept there for the entire drive. Norah and Ingrid counted transport trucks and read their books. Halfway home, Laurel stopped at a gas station and bought sandwiches wrapped in plastic and a tin of tuna for Puss. He ate it quickly, right out of the can, and fell asleep again. For the rest of the drive, the car smelled like tuna.

Ada emerged from the office when she heard the car.

What happened? Ada said when she saw Norah's bandaged foot, and Norah told her the story, showed her the finger puppet. Then Puss hopped out of the car and Norah scooped him up into her arms.

And who's this? Ada said.

Our new cat, Puss, Norah said. Can we keep him?

It seems like he has already made that decision for me, Ada said.

The three of them went into the breakfast room, Norah leaning on Ada's arm and Puss trotting along behind. Ingrid followed the cat, who acted as if he had belonged there all along. Ingrid sat with Ada and Norah at the table by the piano and Puss curled up underneath Norah's chair and went to sleep again. Even as he slept, the cat purred.

CHAPTER 13

Lewes

I spend a lot of time sleeping, alternating between Julia's bed and my room at Susan's. At Julia's, if I leave the window open, I can hear people as they walk by on the sidewalk below, and the muffled sound of their voices and footsteps comforts me. At Susan's, the music from the pub across the street keeps me awake. I avoid phone calls from Laurel, neglect text messages from Elena, stop checking my email and social media. I want to be able to read, but every time I take a book from the pile, I end up holding it unopened.

The smell of hyacinths is already heavy in the air. Cheerful yellow daffodils bob their heads in time to the wind, all facing south. When Julia and I finish work for the day, we go for walks around town to look at the flowers. She points out all the ones she knows and lowers her face to smell them. In a park, I covertly pick two purple hyacinths and hide them in my tote bag. Their smell lingers around us and we hurry home to put them in a vase.

At my cleaning jobs, I usually wear headphones and listen to music. But I can't bring myself to do that anymore because it makes me want to sing along. So instead I turn on the radio, if the place has one, and tune it to the classical station. I don't recognize all the pieces, but when one comes on that I know, I pretend it's Norah playing in the other room. I like the satisfaction of cleaning, how the homes and apartments I work in smell fresh by the time I'm done. Towels neatly folded, mantels dusted, carpets vacuumed, counters wiped down. I work methodically through each room and when I lock the door of each place behind me, I think of the travellers arriving, walking in and commenting on how clean it smells.

The only other things that keep me from thinking too much are watching Julia make pottery, walking, and swimming. One afternoon, after I finish cleaning for the day, I walk to Julia's and sit in her shed to watch her at the wheel. It's hypnotizing, the way the wheel spins. When she concentrates, she bites the side of her lip. The way she turns a lump of clay into a bowl or cup or plate seems like a magic trick.

Want to try? Julia says when I arrive and take up my post on a rickety wooden milking stool. I shake my head, but she insists and gets up from her stool, comes over and takes my hand.

You'll like it, she says. I promise.

I sit behind the wheel and Julia hands me a lump of soft red clay. It's heavy in my hands, and she stands behind me and helps me centre it on the wheel. At first, the wheel moves too fast and my hands shake. But Julia puts her hands over mine to help me shape a small bowl. It takes twice as long as it would've taken her, but as she shows me how to sponge the extra water out and use a wire to get the bowl off the wheel, I'm proud of my rough attempt.

It's perfect, Julia says, holding it up. Now we let it dry and then you can glaze it and I'll put it in the kiln.

The clay on my skin is already starting to dry and harden, making my hands feel leathery. I wash them off at the garden hose while Julia cleans up in the shed. In mid-afternoon the beds full of crocuses, daffodils, and tulips are in partial sun.

Let's go away at the weekend, Julia says as she joins me in the garden. Not very far. We haven't gone to Charleston in a bit.

I nod and hold the hose so Julia can wash her hands too, then I point it into the air over our heads so the water falls down on us like rain.

———

We book a room in a local pub and catch the train on Saturday morning. Lewes Station is quiet, and as we find a bench on the platform I look out towards the white chalk cliffs. Julia goes into The Runaway to get coffee and muffins for the journey and returns just as the train is pulling in.

Taking the window seat, I stare out at the trees and fields flying past, while Julia flips through a magazine. Ever since my visit to the doctor, I've felt like I'm moving in slow motion. Even on a moving train, with the landscape rushing by, the sensation remains. I rest my head on Julia's shoulder and close my eyes.

Julia nudges me awake at Berwick Station. Since we're only booked for one night, we've both packed light, so we walk to the pub from the station. Mist is still rising from the fields and the sheep look like cotton balls stuck in the grass. We check into our room, drop our backpacks on the bed, and leave again almost immediately for Charleston. If you hike high enough into the hills, you can glimpse the sea on a clear day. When I first moved here, I explored the Downs on foot almost every weekend, but

I haven't gone on many long walks recently.

I like being out early in the morning, when the only people around are walkers with their dogs who run ahead with sticks in their mouths. I focus on the sound of our feet on the path, the strangely tropical trilling of the English blackbird, Julia's braid swinging back and forth as she walks. A long dirt lane with deep ruts from farm equipment leads from the main road up to Charleston. So many people have walked up this very same lane over the years. How scared they must have been during the war, with planes flying over and so much uncertainty. Virginia Woolf traipsed across the Downs with her walking stick and her dogs, coming to visit her sister on a Saturday morning just like this one. The house appears, its stone facade partially covered with wild foliage. I love everything about the house, from the soft pink front door to the secret courtyard, which is off-limits to visitors but contains a small pool. The walled garden is overflowing with flowers and there are statues and busts hiding everywhere, peering out at visitors from among the trees and bushes. The floating woman statue by the pond is my favourite, on the far side of the water. Her hair falls to one side; it almost looks like she's resting on the tips of it. The first time I saw her, it was like seeing a ghost.

The place is busy, especially in spring, because everyone enjoys walking through the garden and the orchard. Julia and I purchase our tickets for a self-guided tour, which means we can linger in each room. I like to take my time, absorb the views from the windows and the colours of the fabrics and paint. The place still smells faintly of turpentine and old books, as if the family has stepped out into town and will be back soon for lunch. Maybe we passed them in the lane as we approached the house.

Inside the front door, the main hallway is dark, the walls lined with framed paintings. I like to start in the studio because it's my favourite, with high ceilings and doors that open to the walled garden. It was Duncan Grant's studio, Vanessa having set one up for herself in the attic. Stepping into the main floor studio is like stepping outside. The ceiling opens up above you and light pours in from high windows. Squished tubes of paint lie on top of a wooden dresser and there's an unframed canvas on the easel. Seeing the house for the first time three years ago, I understood why Laurel loved reading about it so much. One day I hope she'll be able to save enough money for a visit with me. I like to picture Laurel seeing these intricate, cozy rooms, and every time I visit, I try to see it through her eyes.

CHAPTER 14

Prince Edward Island, 2004 to 2006

Puss had been living at the Blue Moth for more than a year when Ada announced that he was not earning his keep. She had found baby mice living in the wall of the breakfast room. Guests had complained about strange scuffling noises in the walls, so Ada cut a square out of the drywall behind the refrigerator. It was a Saturday morning in early September. Ingrid and Norah were playing around on the piano. Ada reached into the hole with her gloved hand and scooped out a nest of dryer lint, grass, and hair. Inside the bundle, a dozen squirming pink bodies. Ada held them out for the girls to see, cradled in her palms like an egg.

Can we keep them? Norah said. They can live in a shoebox under my bed.

Ada snorted. That cat may be useless, she said, but he's not that useless. I have a feeling they wouldn't last very long.

She suggested that the three of them take the nest down to

the tall grass by the firepit and leave it there. As they walked, Ada told the girls that within a few minutes a bird would probably swoop down and scoop up the nest, babies and all, to take home to its own children. The girls had watched enough wildlife documentaries on TV to know Ada wasn't making this up, but they looked at the tiny pink creatures and hoped that maybe it wouldn't happen. It seemed like Ada was hoping it too.

This can be our little secret, Ada said as she set the nest down in the grass. No one has to know.

But one of the guests had seen them leaving the breakfast room with the nest of mice and put in a complaint to the health inspector, who arrived the next day and closed down the Blue Moth until the mouse problem was dealt with. He called it a "rodent problem," which seemed more sinister somehow than a "mouse problem." With his clipboard and gruff, deep voice, he was an unwelcome visitor and insisted on searching all the rooms. By the end of the week, all the guests were gone.

Ada told the girls they would have to take a break from music lessons for a week while she figured out what to do. She was always dressed in her best clothes, sharply pressed, with a scarf tied around her hair or neck. Ingrid and Norah continued to practise their music after school, with Puss curled up under the piano bench. They wanted to show Ada they were still dedicated.

The girls had just started Grade Seven, and middle school was a whole different experience from elementary. They had to adapt to new classrooms, new classmates, and a new music room. Norah missed the old piano, but quickly grew attached to the new one. The girls befriended the music teacher, Ms. Winter, who let them spend their recess and lunch in the music room as long as they promised not to play too loudly. She left the door unlocked for the girls so it was easy for them to slip in unnoticed.

There was a boy in their class, John, who took a liking to

Ingrid and started to follow the girls around. He wanted to know what they were doing, where they were going, but they never told him. One day, just after the bell rang for recess, he tried to give Ingrid a present. It was a stuffed animal with big, creepy glass eyes and sparkly purple feet. Ingrid couldn't figure out what type of animal it was supposed to be. She held it awkwardly in her hands.

Now you're my girlfriend, John said, smiling with all his teeth.

Ingrid didn't want to be anyone's girlfriend, especially not John's. She shoved the stuffed animal back into his arms and he stumbled backwards a few steps.

I am not your girlfriend, Ingrid said. I don't even know you.

A group of their classmates were still milling around near the exit. The boys laughed while the girls looked down at their shoes, embarrassed on Ingrid's behalf, or maybe envious.

Mrs. Parkes, the biology teacher, came out of her classroom, clapped her hands twice, and told everyone to get outside. The herd of kids jostled each other on their way out, and Ingrid and Norah broke off and made their way to the music room.

Norah took her place at the piano. Ingrid paced around the room, touching all the music stands and absently flipping through the songbooks.

Can you sit still? Norah said.

Ingrid sat in a tiny plastic chair, tilting it back onto its two back legs.

You were kind of mean to John, Norah said.

I was not. I just told him the truth.

You could've been nicer about it, Norah said as she started to play.

Ingrid stormed out of the room and slammed the door behind her. The noise echoed in the hallway as she started to run, her feet slapping the linoleum. She didn't know where she was going.

At the end of the hallway, she ran out the back door of the school and into the wooded area that was off-limits. It was surrounded by a fence, but there was a place where you could peel the chain-link back and slip through. Ingrid liked to think she was the only one who knew about it, but she had seen cigarette butts and gum wrappers scattered among the roots and dead leaves. There was a pine tree with low branches that was easy to climb, and Ingrid had started to think of it as her tree. It was easier to think when she was high off the ground.

She slipped through the fence and ran to her tree. Swinging on the bottom branch, she gained enough momentum to wrap her legs around it and pull herself up. Her clothes would be covered in sap, but she didn't care. All she wanted to do was climb as high as she could and sit there until she felt less angry. The tree reminded her of the ones she had climbed in Nova Scotia at the campground, and as she climbed higher she wondered if they would go on another family vacation.

About three-quarters of the way up the tree, Ingrid stopped. The branches were getting wobbly, so she chose the thickest one and sat on it, leaning her back against the trunk. She could still see the schoolyard through the branches. A few of her class-mates were running around like disorganized ants while the rest stood in groups or sat on the soccer field. The teacher on duty stood near the door. Ingrid picked a few pine needles off a branch and rubbed them between her palms. A little while later, the bell rang and Ingrid watched all the little ants march back inside. Even though Ingrid knew Norah would look for her and worry when she didn't show up, she made no move to climb down the tree. She liked it up there, closer to the sky, in a world that smelled of sap.

Exterminators went through all the rooms at the Blue Moth to get rid of the mice, and for two nights Ingrid, Norah, Laurel, and Elena had to stay with Ada at her bungalow. The girls had visited the bungalow for family suppers and holiday breakfasts, but this was the first time they'd ever stayed over. They were surprised when Ada showed them a set of new bunk beds in Laurel's old room, and a new desk to go with them, under the window, across from the full bookshelf. She had fixed up a space just for them. The walls were painted lilac and everything else was white. White duvets, a white chair by the desk, sheer white curtains to diffuse the morning sun. Laurel would take the top bunk because Elena had volunteered to sleep on the sofa. The girls would share the bottom.

Ada made tuna casserole and Laurel opened a bottle of red wine before supper was ready. The girls were in the living room, Norah softly playing Ada's old upright piano while Ingrid lay on her stomach on the carpet doing a sudoku, pretending not to listen to the conversation in the kitchen. Laurel sat at the round kitchen table and poured a glass of wine as Elena and Ada peeled apples for dessert. They stood side by side at the counter by the sink.

The mice will be gone by next week, Laurel said. I don't understand why you don't want to reopen right away.

Ada, with her back to her daughter, said the timing wasn't right. No one will book anyway. It's best to wait.

Your mom knows what she's doing, Elena said as she dropped a coil of peel into a paper bag. Let's just trust her, okay?

Laurel sighed and didn't answer. She began to set the table in the dining room, which opened into the living room via an archway.

Come help me set the table, Ingrid, Laurel said.

Norah stood up from the piano bench. I can help too.

Come help in here, Norah, Ada called from the kitchen. You can choose a CD.

Norah looked at her mother, who nodded, so Norah stepped into the kitchen and began looking through Ada's collection, which she kept in a drawer under the CD player. Laurel gave Ingrid a handful of cutlery and a fork clattered to the floor. A few moments later, the voice of Etta James floated through the air, and just like that the mood changed. Ingrid recovered the dropped fork and arranged the cutlery on the placemats. Laurel filled the water glasses, lit three candles in their brass holders, and put the bottle of wine in the centre of the table.

The bungalow, though small and dated, was carefully decorated. This included Ada's bedroom, the girls imagined, though the door was always shut and they had never seen inside. The bungalow was carpeted in pale beige, except for the kitchen and bathroom, which had white linoleum floors. An electric fireplace in the living room emitted a soft glow. The sofa and chair were overstuffed and a few framed Impressionist prints were arranged salon-style on the wall, along with a couple of photographs. Ingrid had always wondered where the pictures came from, especially a faded four-by-six photograph of two young women standing outside a large church. She assumed one of the women was Ada, but she wasn't sure.

Right now, Ada was dishing the casserole onto porcelain plates. She took her place at the head of the table, closest to the kitchen. Etta James continued to sing as forks scraped against china and no one spoke. Ingrid gulped her water loudly.

Where will we live if the Blue Moth closes forever? Ingrid said finally, and Norah kicked her leg.

That won't happen, Laurel said.

You'll live here, Ada said at the same time, and mother and daughter looked at each other across the table. Laurel refilled her wine glass and moved to top up Elena's, but she shook her head.

We'll just have to play it by ear, Ada said.

The smell of apple crisp wafted into the room as silence descended on the table once again. Laurel's lips were stained lipstick-red from the wine. Ingrid thought her mother looked tired, with purple shadows under her eyes.

Is that you, in that photo on the wall? Ingrid asked Ada.

Yes, Ada said. In another lifetime.

You still look the same, Ingrid said, and Ada laughed.

Enough about me, Ada said quickly. Tell me about school.

Norah jumped in with tales of music class and art and how one of their classmates had climbed out the window during French and run across the soccer field. The conversation stayed light after that, all of them making an effort to keep it that way. Elena dished the dessert out with heaps of whipped cream.

Thank you, Elena, Ada said when Elena sat down again. This crisp is perfect.

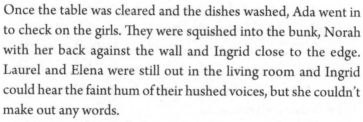

Once the table was cleared and the dishes washed, Ada went in to check on the girls. They were squished into the bunk, Norah with her back against the wall and Ingrid close to the edge. Laurel and Elena were still out in the living room and Ingrid could hear the faint hum of their hushed voices, but she couldn't make out any words.

Would you like a story or a song? Ada asked.

Can we have both? Norah asked.

I don't see why not, she said.

Ingrid thought they were both too old for bedtime stories and songs, but she didn't say anything. Ada stood over by the bookshelf with her back to the girls, scanning the shelves.

Ah, here it is, she said as she pulled down a thick book. She sat on the chair and ran her hand over the book's cover.

This was one of my favourites when I was younger, Ada said. Well, I guess it still is one of my favourites.

She held it up so the girls could see the cover: *Sense and Sensibility*, by Jane Austen.

I always wished I had a sister, Ada said. You two are lucky. This book is about sisters, and Jane Austen also writes a lot about music, so I think you'll both really like it. It's a long book, so we can read a chapter every time you come to visit. Does that sound good?

Ingrid nodded and Norah chirped yes from her blanket cocoon.

Ada started reading. Her voice was low and melodic, and Norah soon fell asleep. But Ingrid was riveted by the story and the way the words sounded different from any other story she had heard. When the first chapter was finished, Ada closed the book and set it on the desk. She softly began to sing "Stay Awake." Her voice was a bit gravelly now, but her pitch was true.

Ada's voice floated down the short hallway to the living room, and made Laurel and Elena stop speaking. It had been a long time since Ada had sung for the joy of it, not since Laurel was very young, before the trucking accident that had killed her dad. He'd driven transport trucks across the country and slept in a bunk in the cab. When Laurel was only seven, his truck hit a guard rail and rolled down a ravine.

When he used to return from a trip, Laurel's dad would come through the door and call out for Ada as Laurel hugged his legs. When Ada appeared, he would lift her off her feet like she weighed nothing and carry her over to the sofa. She'd tell him he was being foolish, to put her down, but she'd be laughing. And then he was gone, just like that, and all the air left the house in one giant breath.

The version of Laurel who had lived in a bungalow with two loving parents had disappeared. But that girl seemed to haunt the place, lurking behind the sofa like a reminder of how things had been and how quickly they had changed. Laurel reached for Elena's hand and leaned against her shoulder as her mother sang.

Ada reduced the girls' music lessons to three times a week because she was busy trying to figure out how to keep the Blue Moth alive. The Bingo nights were still successful, but the number of people attending had started to drop. Even once the mice were gone, Ada decided to wait until late spring to open again. Elena and Laurel found jobs waiting tables at a roadside restaurant. They worked the breakfast shift together and left in the Nissan six days a week, at 4:30 in the morning. Ingrid woke up when she heard the car start and sometimes she stood outside the door and waved as they drove away. They returned in the afternoons smelling of deep-fryer oil and slept until suppertime.

To pass the time during those dark winter evenings, Norah and Ingrid took movies out from the library along with their books. They liked musicals best because they could learn the songs, but they also borrowed movies about kids who went on adventures. Norah especially liked a Japanese one called *Kiki's Delivery Service*, about a thirteen-year-old girl who is a witch and has a talking cat named Jiji. For a little while, Norah even wore a red bow in her hair like Kiki. It was admirable how independent Kiki was, how she set out at age thirteen to discover a new life.

Every weekend Ada took the girls to the pub for their gig. They still saved their money in the Mason jars, but Ada had decided they were old enough to get bank accounts. One day she picked them up at school in her blue Cadillac, with a bench seat in the front that was big enough for three. Norah claimed the window seat and Ingrid perched in the middle. On the way into the city, they all sang along to the radio. Ingrid intentionally sang quieter than usual so Ada's voice floated above. Norah slid into harmony.

At the bank, the girls received debit cards and wrote their names in cursive on the back. They left the building carrying their empty Mason jars. Ingrid looked at her card and tried to associate the plastic with all that hard-earned money. Back in the car, Ada presented the girls with wallets she had bought for them to keep their cards safe.

You can keep your library cards in there too, Ada said.

The wallets were covered in blue sparkles that looked like fish scales. On the drive home, Ingrid thought about what she could do with her now-empty Mason jar. Grow crystals on strings or store nuts and seeds for the seagulls. But Norah had other ideas.

We can use them to catch the moths so we can look at them. Just for minute, she said. If they ever come back.

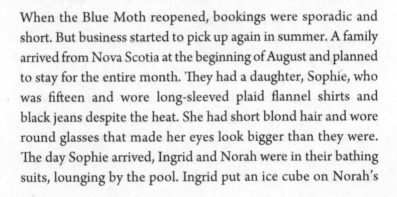

When the Blue Moth reopened, bookings were sporadic and short. But business started to pick up again in summer. A family arrived from Nova Scotia at the beginning of August and planned to stay for the entire month. They had a daughter, Sophie, who was fifteen and wore long-sleeved plaid flannel shirts and black jeans despite the heat. She had short blond hair and wore round glasses that made her eyes look bigger than they were. The day Sophie arrived, Ingrid and Norah were in their bathing suits, lounging by the pool. Ingrid put an ice cube on Norah's stomach, and Norah shrieked, leaped up, and chased Ingrid around the pool deck until she caught her and pushed her into the water.

Sophie stood beside her parents' car and watched. Ingrid noticed her when she entered the pool area through the gate and hovered next to a lawn chair in her heavy boots. Ingrid propped herself up at the edge of the pool.

Hey, Ingrid said.

Hey. I'm Sophie.

Cool. I'm Ingrid, that's my sister, Norah.

From the other side of the pool, Norah waved.

She's a bit shy, Ingrid said.

That's cool.

I like your boots, Ingrid said. Want to swim with us?

Sophie nodded. She disappeared for a few minutes, returned in a black one-piece suit, and did a cannonball into the pool. When she surfaced, Ingrid and Norah both cheered.

What grade are you in? Ingrid asked as they treaded water.

Starting Grade Ten in September. She smoothed back her hair so it looked like a swim cap. High school, she said.

We're starting Grade Eight, Norah said, and at the same time Ingrid blurted out, I can't wait for high school.

I'm going to join the swim team, Sophie said. Want to race me?

Ingrid accepted the challenge. Norah said she would watch to make sure the race was fair. She pulled herself out of the water and sat at the end of the pool.

On your mark, get set, go! Norah called, and Sophie and Ingrid pushed off from the other end like rockets. Sophie's arms moved rhythmically and fast, her legs a blur, and she quickly pulled ahead. Norah splashed her feet in the water for encouragement, and when Sophie touched the end first, she clapped. Ingrid arrived a few moments later, out of breath and spluttering.

You win! Ingrid said. You're really fast.

Sophie wiped the water from her eyes.

So, what else do you do around here? Sophie asked.

The rest of the summer passed in a blur. The girls had never had a friend before. Sophie loved the beach—they splashed in the waves for hours, ran back and forth across the sand in search of driftwood to jump over. On Sundays, she went into the city with them and clapped the loudest at their set in the pub.

You're both going to be famous someday, Sophie said in the car on the way back to the Blue Moth one Sunday. And I'll be able to say I knew you when.

The girls showed Sophie the piano and told her the story of the moths. Puss took a liking to her and sometimes sat outside the room where she was staying, waiting to be let inside. In the evenings, after supper, Norah tried to teach Sophie how to play the piano, and by the end of the summer she could manage a slowed-down version of *"Für Elise."*

They had a few sleepovers at Ada's bungalow and stayed up late eating candy until their tastebuds were sore. They rented movies and took turns choosing what to watch. The girls let Sophie have the top bunk. Ada made berry smoothies in the mornings and they all sat together in the kitchen.

Sophie carried a small shoulder bag. Ingrid wasn't brave enough to ask what was inside. About halfway through the month, it was Norah who finally voiced the question, and Sophie opened the bag and showed them its contents. A lighter, in case she got lost in the woods, extra shoelaces for her boots, a few dollars in change, a package of bubble gum, some comic strips she had cut out of the newspaper, a tampon, a few hair elastics from when she used to have long hair, a pencil and pad of paper.

Business had picked up a bit at the Blue Moth. Laurel and Elena kept their jobs at the roadside restaurant but switched to afternoon shifts so they could clean the occupied rooms. Ingrid and Norah barely saw them all summer, especially once Sophie had arrived.

At the end of August, when Sophie and her parents had to leave, the girls promised to keep in touch. Sophie rolled down her window as the car pulled out of the courtyard.

See you next summer! she hollered.

Ingrid and Norah watched the car until it disappeared. They stood side by side in the empty courtyard.

The girls logged on to the computer in the office every day to see if Sophie was also online. When she was, they talked until Ada kicked them out. Sophie made the high school swim team and had to train for two hours every morning before school started. Her hair was tinged green from the chlorine, she said, but she didn't mind. But as fall turned into winter, Sophie was harder to get hold of. They chatted a few times around Christmas, and Sophie put pictures of their faces in a funny e-card of elves doing a dance. And then there was nothing after that.

For the first time ever, Ada had to coax the girls into the breakfast room to practise their music. Once they got started they were as enthusiastic as ever, but when they were checking online for Sophie it was as if they were in a trance. Ada said maybe Sophie's family had moved, and Sophie would probably log on again once they were settled.

If she does come back this summer, can we have another Blue Moth Extravaganza? Norah asked.

Even though it was spring, the world felt static and lifeless. Ingrid had never been so bored. Business at the Blue Moth had taken another dip, and the girls often saw Laurel, Elena, and Ada sitting around the desk in the office bent over papers. Ingrid tried to hover by the door to listen, but Norah pulled her along to the breakfast room and played the piano loudly, fingers flying.

They were waiting, but they didn't really know what for. Waiting for the Blue Moth to get busy again. For Sophie to re-appear. During that long Grade Eight spring, the air at the Blue Moth felt charged and the adults walked around with bags under their eyes. Norah played the piano until her fingers ached and Ingrid started drinking lemon tea to soothe her throat from so much singing. But she tried, unsuccessfully, to convince Norah to go busking downtown. They continued with their weekly pub gig, did a couple of funerals, and continued saving money in their bank accounts. At the library, they flipped through travel books and planned the places they would go when they were old enough to travel on their own. Even though Norah thought they were too old to play games anymore, Ingrid still insisted on Around the World. She closed her eyes as her fingers moved over the smooth surface of the globe and she pictured all the new scenery and streets and people.

All the girls at school were at the age where they had to figure out how to inhabit their bodies. Ingrid watched as they stood outside the chain-link fence around the basketball court, waiting for some boy to notice them. They fixed each other's hair, shared lip gloss, and wore clothes that were either too loose or too tight. Band T-shirts borrowed from older siblings, tattered canvas shoes they drew on with markers during class, low-rise jeans. Ingrid wondered why they smudged so much dark makeup around their eyes; it made them look scared and pale rather than nonchalant and carefree. Most of the girls seemed to walk the same way, with languid limbs, as if they had just woken up from a nap.

But as soon as they were on their own, no longer on display, they transformed. In the locker room, they were loud and excited, all arms and legs and swinging hair. They laughed and didn't cover their mouths. Locker doors slammed, shoes squeaked, clothes were balled up and tossed across the room, hair elastics ricocheted off the walls. Ingrid liked them better when they were like that, awkward and gangly, because that was how she felt all the time.

In late May, the girls received a message from Sophie.

She'd been busy and hadn't been able to log on in a while; she had a boyfriend named Tom who owned a car and drove her anywhere she wanted to go. And her parents had finally agreed to return to the Blue Moth—they'd be coming for two weeks at the end of June. When the girls read that, they ran to find Ada, who was at her desk. Her chin was resting in her hand and her eyes were unfocused when the girls arrived. They talked over each other, jostling in their eagerness to get through the doorway.

Hold on, hold on, Ada said as she stood up slowly.

Are you okay? Norah said.

Yes, yes, I'm fine, Ada said. Let's go sit in the breakfast room.

Ingrid bounded ahead while Norah held back and took Ada's arm. They sat at their usual table and the girls told Ada about Sophie's message. The words were hardly out of their mouths— talking over each other again—when Ada nodded her head in agreement. Yes, they could have another Blue Moth Extravaganza in honour of Sophie's return.

CHAPTER 15

Lewes

At Charleston, Julia and I sit on a bench by the pond in front of the house. Sun is starting to peek through the mist, and the car park—a large field down the lane—is filling up. People walk towards the house and pause to take pictures with their phones as it comes into view. Photographs aren't allowed inside, so they take full advantage now. Julia takes my hand, her skin dry from clay, and I stare at the statue of the floating lady almost hidden in the trees on the far side of the pond. How many of the visitors notice her? Every time I come to Charleston, I see something different. I like to think about what the house was like when it was still a home. It's still a living, breathing place, full of detail and light, but it feels partially frozen, as if waiting for its former occupants to return.

I miss the Blue Moth, but mostly I miss the child I was there. I used to dream about all the houses I might live in, all the people I could be. All those notebooks full of lists of places Norah and I planned to visit. I've managed to make it across the ocean but nowhere else. People talk about how easy it is to travel between the UK and other places in Europe, but I've never been able to get the time off work or save enough money. I dream of seeing the caldera of Santorini and vineyards in Italy, but they're still dreams. For now, visiting Charleston is how I travel.

Julia rubs her thumb in circles on the back of my hand and looks out over the pond. I want to pull my hand away, but I don't.

We sit on the bench for a bit longer, listening to the birds. I want to go inside the house again and hide in one of the rooms until the rest of the visitors leave. Maybe if I wait long enough, everyone will come back.

CHAPTER 16

Prince Edward Island, 2006

Norah designed posters for The Blue Moth Extravaganza. The girls put them up at school and all around the city. Norah's bold design—a large blue moth with all the details written in its wings—drew the eye. Her artistic ability had improved greatly over the years since her first poster design. The phone number of the Blue Moth was written in bold red ink at the bottom in Norah's tidy block letters. Every day while they waited for Sophie to arrive, Norah and Ingrid sat in the office by the phone. On the calendar on the wall next to Ada's desk, they crossed off each square when they left for the evening.

When Norah answered the phone, she changed her voice in a way that made it sound like Laurel's when she was frustrated with Ingrid for not making the beds properly or for wearing the same shirt two days in a row. The formal edge to Norah's quiet tone made her sound older. In between calls, which were few, the girls did their homework, read, or played games with a deck of cards from Ada's desk drawer.

At ten o'clock, it was time for bed. No one ever called that late, but the girls stayed in the office just in case. The pool had reopened in early June with the gurgle that signified the beginning of summer. At a certain time every evening, when the sun was just right, the reflection from the water rippled on the ceiling of the office, making the room feel as if it was under the sea. Ingrid lay on the carpet and stared upwards.

Do you know how many people have walked across that floor with their dirty shoes? Norah sounded very much like Laurel. You're probably lying in dog poop.

School let out for the summer a week before The Blue Moth Extravaganza. Ingrid and Norah talked about the party and wondered if the moths would come. Out by the pool, Ada slept in a lounge chair with her sunglasses on. Puss alternated between sleeping under her chair and lying under the desk in the office with the girls, who watched Ada through the window. Sometimes she didn't move for hours. Norah would go check on her, carrying a glass of lemon water with ice. When the ice melted, beads of condensation dripped down the sides of the glass, making a water ring on the plastic table.

The girls came across papers filled with numbers and confusing details about the Blue Moth. Norah read them as though she were studying for an exam and tried to interpret their contents. From what the girls could figure out, the Blue Moth had been on the brink of bankruptcy for a long time and Ada was struggling to pay the taxes and keep up with the other bills. Somehow, Ada was just managing to keep the men in suits away from the door.

No way would Ada have let the girls buy the food for the party with their own money, so they didn't tell her. They went to the grocery store and bought hamburgers, hot dogs, and buns. S'mores kits were on sale, so they bought a few of those too. Even though the Blue Moth was still surviving, the girls believed the party had to be a success in order to prove to people that it was still a place worth going to.

The tea lights they had used before to line the path from the motel to the gazebo no longer worked, so the girls bought new ones at the dollar store and made tissue-paper lanterns to put around them. They covered the floor of their room with the lanterns and were surrounded by a sea of soft blue light. Ingrid wondered if that was what it would look like if the moths arrived with their iridescent blue wings flickering in the grass.

The day before the party, Norah and Ingrid walked into the city to go shopping at the thrift store. Ingrid wanted to wear a tie and white shirt with high-waisted pants and a long coat, like an archaeologist on an expedition. The girls had recently watched *Raiders of the Lost Ark*. Norah wanted to wear a silk scarf around her neck. They tried on outfits in the fitting rooms and Ingrid looked at herself in the full-length mirror. Her chest was still flat; her hip bones jutted out. She turned sideways and searched for some hint of a curve, arched her back so her stomach and chest stuck out.

In the fitting room mirror, Ingrid looked at her sister with envy as Norah swept her hair over one shoulder and dipped her head forward so Ingrid could zip up her dress. She'd chosen a long cotton dress with small blue flowers against a white background. The sleeves were puffed at the shoulders. With a square neck and full skirt, it was very flattering, and Norah smoothed her hands over the front of it.

Ingrid found her clothes in the men's section. Norah convinced her not to buy a tie, but to use a floral scarf instead. The pop of colour brightened the otherwise pale outfit. The girls left with their old clothes in plastic bags and walked back across the Hillsborough bridge in their new ones. The way the trench coat billowed behind her made Ingrid feel like a character in a different story, even though it was a bit too warm for the weather.

In the evening, Laurel drove the girls back into the city to pick up the flowers they had ordered. Carnations and roses dyed pale blue, exploding zinnias and hydrangeas also in shades of blue. The humid air in the florist's shop was like stepping into a tropical rainforest. Ingrid wanted to stay there forever, touching the ferns and breathing in the green. The flowers were for the tables in the breakfast room, where everyone would go for the entertainment portion of the evening.

Ingrid woke up on the morning of the party terrified that no one would come. She crawled out of bed, leaving Norah sleeping soundly, and crossed the courtyard to the breakfast room in her bare feet. She sat on the piano bench and placed her fingers lightly on the keys. Norah said when she played it was as if energy radiated off the piano through her fingers and into her body. Norah looked so serene when she played, and Ingrid was afraid she didn't look nearly that beautiful when she was singing. She played a few notes, but she didn't have anything memorized and had to flip through the songbook.

Footsteps sounded in the courtyard and Ingrid looked over her shoulder to see Ada step through the doorway. Her eyes looked tired, but she brightened when she saw the flowers on the tables.

Today's the day, she said.

Ingrid helped Ada with the breakfast and some time later Norah appeared, still in her pajamas. She sat down on the piano bench and began to play even though she was still half asleep.

After breakfast, Norah and Ingrid draped blue streamers around the room and blew up balloons until they were light-headed. Elena and Laurel did their morning rounds, then they helped by lining the pathway to the gazebo with the tissue-paper lanterns. The day was filled with the possibility of the moths.

When Sophie and her parents arrived around lunchtime, the girls ran to greet her. Their friend was a little bit taller than last year, and her hair was longer, grazing her chin. The three of them sat by the pool, dangling their feet in the water. The sun beat down on their shoulders and Ingrid knew her skin was burning but she didn't care. She didn't want to take the time to put on sunscreen. As Sophie talked about her boyfriend and the swim team and high school, Ingrid realized how much had changed in Sophie's life and how little had changed in her own. She still lived in the same room, still slept in the same bed with her sister, still wore a lot of the same clothes she had always worn. It was as if the walls of the Blue Moth were shrinking, the sky pressing down on her head, holding her in place.

Ingrid jumped to her feet and leaped into the pool, fully clothed. With a loud whoop, Sophie jumped in too, and Norah followed. Their clothes billowed out around them like curtains and droplets of water glittered in the sun.

Later, once everything was decorated, the girls went to their room to get changed. Laurel and Elena were already inside getting dressed and doing their hair. Envious of Ingrid's curls, Norah asked Elena to use the curling iron on her hair. She sat on the floor as Elena sat on the edge of the bed and carefully gave her straight blond hair some curl. Ingrid decided to let her own hair go wild, rather than trying to contain it in a braid. Explorers didn't have time to worry about such things.

The girls wanted their outfits to be a surprise, so they changed in the bathroom and made Laurel and Elena close their eyes until they emerged and said Ta-da!

You both look very much like your true selves, Laurel said,

and the girls grinned. In her high-waisted pants and trench coat, Ingrid realized clothes had that power. Norah twirled to show how the full skirt moved.

Around five o'clock, the girls lit the tissue-paper lanterns. The sun was still bright, but in the story Laurel had told them, the moths always swarmed at dusk; the girls didn't want to miss them. Elena and Laurel went down to the gazebo to organize the food and start the bonfire, and once all the lanterns were lit, Ingrid and Norah returned to the courtyard to greet the guests.

Sophie was waiting by the pool wearing a dark green cotton dress. The three of them talked excitedly and waited for guests to arrive, eating sour candy Sophie had brought for them. As the first few guests trickled in, the girls directed them down the path towards the bonfire. At seven o'clock there was still no sign of Ada. Ingrid was hungry, so she went down to the fire to get something to eat; Sophie and Norah followed a short time later.

A guy who worked at the gas station next door had brought his guitar. He sat cross-legged in the grass by the fire strumming an unfamiliar tune, with a hot dog balanced on one knee. Ingrid sat at a picnic table eating a veggie burger off a Styrofoam plate and drinking Coke out of a red plastic cup. A few kids from school had come with their parents, and it was strange to see them out of the context of the classroom. They looked less intimidating, more hesitant, standing next to their families, eating hot dogs. The adults took in the paper lanterns, the gazebo by the water, the roaring fire, and the view of the city across the harbour. The Blue Moth looked more charming at night, when it was too dark to see the faded siding and the cracks in the pavement. The goal of the party was to show everyone that the Blue Moth Motel wasn't the rodent-infested, rundown place people seemed to think it was. As long as half the rooms were filled that summer, the men in suits would stay away.

Norah and Ingrid hadn't told anyone about the fireworks. They'd set them up on the little strip of beach the day before and asked one of the employees from the gas station to light them at dusk. As the bonfire burned down to hot coals, Elena handed out sticks and passed around a bag of marshmallows. Ingrid crouched down next to the bonfire and toasted her marshmallow until it was evenly brown. She peeled off the skin and ate the sugary inside right off the stick.

By eight o'clock, Ada still had not appeared. A few people had gone back to the courtyard and were milling around the pool. Bits of their laughter drifted all the way to the gazebo. As the sky faded to purple, Norah, Ingrid, and Sophie began their search for the moths. They walked slowly through the grass looking for any sign of movement. After a few minutes of searching, Norah grabbed Ingrid's arm. Look, she said, and pointed.

Ada was walking along the lantern-lined pathway in her blue chiffon dress with a matching blue scarf tied around her hair. The glow from the tea lights illuminated the fabric of the dress as it billowed out behind her. As she got closer, the girls ran to her. The chiffon wrapped around them like a curtain and the world turned blue.

———

Ada had strung fairy lights around the windows and over the piano in the breakfast room. When Norah sat on the bench, she glowed under the lights. Ingrid took her place behind the microphone while the guests filed in and took their seats. With the sun going down, there was a chill in the air, so some of the guests had draped blankets over their summer dresses or put on hooded sweatshirts.

Ingrid sang and swayed with the music. She had wanted to

do a popular song for their finale—something by Mariah Carey or Shakira—but Norah had insisted on sticking with the songs they knew best.

Now Norah whispered in her sister's ear that she had a classical piece she wanted to perform on her own. So Ingrid stepped away from the microphone and Norah took her place.

I wrote this piece of music for someone who is very important to me and the Blue Moth, Norah said. Without her, I wouldn't have discovered the piano. So this is for Ada.

As Norah returned to the piano bench, she looked out at the expectant faces.

This piece is called "The Blue Moth," she said.

Ingrid went offstage and stood with Sophie. It was the first time Norah had performed without her sister, but if she was nervous, she was hiding it well. The piece began slowly. As she played, Norah leaned into the music. Her dress was spread out around her on the piano bench, and with the curls in her hair she looked like someone new. The music sped up, became slightly ominous. Ingrid wondered if that was the energy Norah talked about. She had put so much of herself into the piece that her body alone wasn't enough to contain all the energy radiating from the music. Each note swarmed into the air and beat its wings.

When the song ended, there was a long moment of silence. Then Ada stepped towards the piano and clapped. Everyone joined in, and the applause continued for a long time. Guests spilled out into the courtyard and Ada joined Norah at the piano. They began to play a duet, the music floating out into the courtyard. The sky was dark enough for the fireworks, so Ingrid slipped away and ran down to the beach to tell the boy from the gas station to light them.

When she made it down the crumbling sandstone bank to the sliver of beach, the boy was nowhere to be seen, but the fireworks were still standing in the sand. Ingrid climbed back up the bank and found the barbecue lighter in the gazebo. It was so quiet down by the water, the waves lapping gently at the shore. Ingrid listened to their rhythm, like a repeating beat. With the lighter, she carefully ignited the first of the fireworks. As they shot into the air and exploded over the water, she heard shrieks of delight from the guests by the pool. She lit the fireworks in careful order, a choreographed show, and saved the best ones for last. As they shot into the sky, Ingrid stood back and watched until the last of the smoke faded away.

By the time the last guests departed, the girls were exhausted. They collapsed on top of the covers, still wearing their party clothes, and Ingrid fell asleep almost immediately. But Norah remained awake for a little longer, listening. Music was coming from the breakfast room, where Ada sat at the piano and continued to play.

The next morning, the girls knew they had a day of cleaning ahead of them. The paper lanterns needed to be collected, the water in the flower vases refreshed, balloons and streamers taken down from the breakfast room. Ingrid felt Norah shifting around, so she rolled over. What are you doing?

Puss isn't here, Norah said. He's always right here, at my feet.

The door to their room was wide open and Laurel and Elena weren't in their bed. A flashing blue light illuminated the room, pulsing. The girls went out into the courtyard. Puss appeared, circling Norah's legs. An ambulance had its back doors open and a police car was parked nearby. Laurel stood outside the office with her hands over her face. Before Ingrid could say anything, Norah ran.

It was Elena who had called the ambulance. She was the one who found Ada slumped over at a table in the breakfast room. As Norah ran across the courtyard, Laurel came forward and tried to catch her. But Norah was agile; she slipped out of her mother's grasp and ran into the breakfast room. Through the window, Ingrid saw them lift the stretcher. She saw Norah following behind them. Ada was covered completely with a white sheet, her blue dress visible where it hung over the edge.

Ingrid watched as Elena pulled Norah away and led her over to Laurel. The paramedics loaded the stretcher into the back of the ambulance with its flashing lights. Ingrid wanted to go to her family, but she couldn't move. She watched as the ambulance doors closed. One paramedic remained in the back while the other one got behind the wheel. She had blond hair pulled back in a neat bun and Ingrid thought she looked more like a ballerina than a first responder. Ingrid waited for the sirens, but there was no sound. She wished for the deafening scream, the sense of urgency. Ada would be okay. Ingrid wanted the siren to shatter the deafening silence of the courtyard at dawn. The blue and red lights reflected off the windows and the pool and flashed across Laurel and Elena's pale faces. As the ambulance and police car drove out of the courtyard slowly, Norah stepped away from everyone. The light fell on her and for a moment she was illuminated in blue.

CHAPTER 17

Lewes

Julia and I walk through the garden and into the orchard at Charleston. We're the only ones among the apple trees, so we sit in the tall grass underneath one and breathe in the fading scent of the blossoms. The blooms are starting to turn brown, getting ready to begin their transformation into fruit. I'm starting to notice things again, to pay attention to the world outside of myself.

It must have been magical to grow up here, Julia says. But probably very isolated.

I nod, pluck a long blade of grass, and hand it to her. She cups it between her thumbs and whistles. It sounds like a duck. I want to stay under the tree forever. Every day I feel differently about whether or not I want to return to the Blue Moth. What if it isn't the same as I remember?

Do you want to go to the churchyard? Julia asks.

I think for a moment, but finally shake my head. I've yet to visit the place where Vanessa Bell is buried, and for some reason I don't want to. Even though I spent so much of my childhood playing among headstones, they've taken on a different meaning now.

We stand and make our way back through the garden and down the long lane to the main road. I look back at the house as we walk away. The smell of the garden fades; the pond disappears behind the trees. No matter how much time I spend here, it never feels like enough. Even though it's an ocean away from the Blue Moth, visiting Charleston always makes me homesick.

Maybe someday we'll live in a house like that, Julia says.

CHAPTER 18

Prince Edward Island, 2006

There was no funeral or visitation. Ada had written in her will that her body was to be donated to science. She would not be drained of blood and placed in a wooden box. She would not have her name engraved on a thick piece of stone to stand in the cemetery. Ingrid thought about how many hours she and Norah had spent chasing each other between the headstones while Laurel tore up weeds and mowed the grass in neat lines. She looked so much like Ada when she mowed the grass. The girls knew there were people buried under their feet, but the reality of the concept had escaped them, until now.

Norah slept curled up like a seashell. Grief made her small, as if she might disappear. Ingrid kept waking up in the middle of the night after having nightmares about Norah drowning. She was floating in the dark sea in a beam of light, her eyes closed. Ingrid called Norah's name over and over, but she didn't respond. What frightened Ingrid the most was how peaceful her sister looked. As if, even if she heard Ingrid calling, Norah was choosing not to answer.

Sophie and her parents left a few days after the party. Sophie promised to write, but it was hard to know what to say. The girls were awkward with her, uncertain in their grieving. It was all too new.

A week later, Laurel decided the four of them would move into Ada's bungalow. The Blue Moth would remain open for the rest of the summer, but in the fall it would close while Laurel figured out what to do. With Ada gone, the Blue Moth now belonged to Laurel. Ada was there, and then she was gone. And that was death, every time.

———

The four of them packed their most important things and drove to the bungalow. In the car, Puss curled up on Norah's lap and fell asleep with one paw over his eyes. When Laurel parked the Nissan in the driveway, no one got out. The engine ticked and Ingrid stared out the window at the front door. She had dreamed about living in a real house, and now they had one, but it wasn't home. She unclipped her seat belt and got out anyway. Norah hadn't said a word all day, and Laurel's face looked doughy and pale.

Ingrid approached the front door while the others unloaded their bags. It was unlocked and swung open easily. A pile of mail sat on the mat inside the door and the air was heavy from a week of being closed up. Ingrid wandered through the rooms, touching picture frames and glass figurines. Ada was the one who had been keeping them all together. All along, Ingrid thought Laurel had created the world of the Blue Moth, but now she knew it was Ada. Without her, they were adrift.

The room with the bunk beds was dark, blinds shut against the sun. Ingrid sat on the edge of the bottom bunk and leaned forward so her fingers grazed the floor and her head rested on her knees. She listened as everyone else came inside, heard someone in the kitchen open a cupboard and turn on the tap. Norah's feet appeared in the doorway and she dropped her bag next to Ingrid's on the floor. She sat next to her sister.

I won't be able to sleep here, Ingrid said.

That first night in the bungalow, they ate a quick dinner of box mac and cheese in front of the television. They watched the five o'clock news and the six o'clock local news. The tourism season was off to an excellent start and the new coastal drive was on schedule to open. Elena said they should go in the car to check it out, but Laurel said it would be too busy and they should wait until later in the summer.

Around midnight, when the house was quiet, Ingrid and Norah slipped out of bed and put on their shoes and sweaters over their pajamas. There were very few cars on the road at that time of night, and no one noticed them. The walk was long, almost an hour, and they went most of the way in silence. As they entered the courtyard at the Blue Moth, the pool glowed and gurgled as if to welcome them. The girls crept to their room and let themselves in. There, sound asleep in her bed, was Laurel.

Ingrid and Norah froze just inside the door and stared at the sleeping form of their mother. She slept on her side, one arm under the pillow and the other curled under her chin. Quietly, the girls slipped off their shoes and climbed into the bed with her, one on either side.

Ingrid woke near dawn with a heavy pain in her stomach. She lay in bed for a few moments, still half asleep. But her body felt tight and hot, as if something inside wanted out. When she pulled back the covers and saw a small, dark stain on the sheet, she understood what was happening. A couple of months away from her fourteenth birthday, she'd seen girls at school swapping tampons in the locker room. She got up and went into the bathroom.

A few hours later, when Ingrid woke up again and remembered, she pulled back the sheets to look at the stain. She was surprised by how brown and earthy it looked. Rather than a bright, cartoonish red, the colour more closely resembled the sandstone cliffs.

The Blue Moth remained open for now. Laurel worked seven days a week between the restaurant and the Blue Moth, despite Elena's pleas for her to take it easy. On the weekends, Elena and the girls cleaned up the bungalow, dusting and vacuuming and cleaning the bathroom like they were preparing for tourists at the Blue Moth. But Ada's closets remained full, her photo albums untouched, her books still on their shelves. How was one supposed to go about boxing up a life? Living among her things was unbearable too, every item a reminder. Most nights, Laurel still snuck away to sleep at the Blue Moth.

Norah and Ingrid stopped going to their weekly gig at the pub. It reminded them too much of Ada. In the breakfast room at the Blue Moth, the piano sat silent because Norah no longer wanted to play. She offered no explanation, and Ingrid was angry with her sister, angry with everyone, for shutting down. Ingrid still wanted to perform.

In September, the girls were due to start Grade Nine, but Norah refused to go. She said she would rather help out at the Blue Moth and do her school work from home. Laurel called the school and got permission for Norah to complete the year from home.

You don't have to go either, Ingrid, Laurel said. But Ingrid couldn't think of anything worse than spending the entire fall and winter dusting empty rooms and staring at the empty pool. Soon, without the tourists in their bathing suits and straw hats, the Blue Moth would start to resemble an abandoned place, somewhere people had forgotten. And Ingrid kept expecting to see Ada in the breakfast room or at her desk in the office, and every time she saw Norah walk by with Ada's scarf tied around her hair, she turned away. Ingrid thought about the time Ada did a cannonball into the pool and swam with them under the hot sun. How could people disappear from the world just like that, without warning?

On the first day of school, when Ingrid walked through the doors alone, she remembered the very first time she'd ever been there. At the end of Grade Six their class had come for a tour. Their teacher had led them through the halls and handed out paper maps of the school so no one would get lost, while the middle school students gawked at them as if they were a parade. Norah had reached for Ingrid's hand, but she had moved away. They were almost middle school students themselves; it didn't seem right to hold hands like little kids. But now, as Ingrid arrived on her first day of Grade Nine, she wished she could go back to that moment and take Norah's hand.

As always, some kids looked the same as she remembered them, but others seemed to have grown taller, or cooler, since

June. Like they'd entered a different phase. A girl called Kate sat a few desks away from Ingrid in Math and English. Kate wore new clothes and clean white sneakers. It was rumoured that her parents had let her get a real tattoo of a small butterfly on her arm over the summer, but no one had seen it yet. Ingrid didn't care either way, but part of her wanted to walk over to Kate's desk and pull up the sleeve of her crisp pink blouse to confirm the rumour or prove it false.

In the mornings, Ingrid caught the bus alone. She sat near the back and kept her head down. When she arrived at school, some of the other girls disappeared into the washroom to touch up their makeup. They applied thicker layers of eyeliner and shadow, used fluffy brushes to make their cheeks glow pink. This ritual seemed like an acquired skill Ingrid had somehow missed. Some of the eyeshadow they applied had sparkles that caught the light. The way the girls applied the colour reminded Ingrid of painting. She wondered what it would feel like to be able to transform yourself into someone new.

Without Norah, Ingrid ended up spending her free time in the library instead of the music room. She read *To Kill a Mockingbird* and *The Great Gatsby* because they were assigned. A bit of Shakespeare, too, which she enjoyed because it was challenging, like learning a new language. One day at lunch, Ingrid was eating her tuna sandwich in the stacks when she heard the click-clack of high-heeled shoes against linoleum. She shoved the sandwich back into its plastic bag and hid it behind her back, hoping to hide the fish smell. Mrs. Jones, the middle school librarian, hardly ever emerged from behind her desk, and Ingrid was a bit scared of her. But it wasn't Mrs. Jones who appeared at the end of the stacks; it was Mrs. Ricci, who taught French to Ingrid's grade and taught choir and music at the high school. She was wearing a knee-length grey wool skirt, black tights, and a floral blouse. In her hand she held a slim book bound in green fabric. The dust jacket was missing but Ingrid read the title on the spine as Mrs. Ricci held it out: *The Waves*, by Virginia Woolf.

You might like this, too, Mrs. Ricci said.

Ingrid reached up and took the book, flipped it open to the first page. It smelled musty, like it had been sitting unopened on the shelf for a long time. Maybe nobody wanted to read it.

It's not for everyone, Mrs. Ricci said. It's challenging. But you may find it worth it.

Thanks, Ingrid said as she flipped to the first page and started reading. "The sun had not yet risen. The sea was indistinguishable from the sky, except that the sea was slightly creased as if a cloth had wrinkles in it."

When the bell rang for the end of lunch, Ingrid barely heard it. She remained hidden in her spot in the stacks. The sentences were long and dense, unlike anything she had read before. She advanced slowly, sometimes reading a sentence two or three times in order to understand. When she reached page thirty, the school day was over. Ingrid heard the rush of bodies in the hallway outside the library, locker doors slamming, the softer squeaking of sneakers. Reluctantly, she closed the book and slipped it into her backpack. Her head swam with the liquid sentences. Ingrid left the library in a trance and made her way to her locker. The hallways emptied as everyone ran to catch their bus, but Ingrid was unable to move quickly. By the time she stepped outside, the buses had left and the parking lot was almost empty. She sighed, still feeling kind of watery, and sat on a bench next to a garbage can. She took the book out of her bag again, just to look at it.

Do you need a lift? Mrs. Ricci said from somewhere behind her.

Ingrid turned. I missed my bus.

Come on, Mrs. Ricci said.

Mrs. Ricci drove a small hatchback. The interior was pristine and smelled of coconut air freshener. When she turned the key in the ignition, the radio blared and she fumbled to turn it down, apologizing.

I love music, Ingrid said as they pulled out of the parking lot.

Are you in the school band? Mrs. Ricci said.

Ingrid shook her head and turned her face to look out the window. She was grateful when Mrs. Ricci didn't ask why.

I live at the Blue Moth, Ingrid said. Across the bridge. I hope it's not too far out of your way.

I drive by every day, Mrs. Ricci said as she turned the radio up again.

Ingrid resisted the urge to sing along, gripping the book in her lap. She wasn't sure why she'd asked Mrs. Ricci to drive her to the Blue Moth rather than to Ada's bungalow. No matter how hard Ingrid tried to think of the bungalow as home, it never would be. When the car turned into the courtyard, Ingrid saw the cleaning cart full of fresh towels parked outside one of the rooms. The pool was still open, but the days were getting colder and it would have to be closed soon. Ingrid tried to see the place through Mrs. Ricci's eyes, but all she could see was home.

Thanks, Ingrid said as she unclipped her seat belt. For the drive and the book.

See you tomorrow, Mrs. Ricci said.

As Ingrid hopped out of the car, Norah emerged from the motel room with a bag full of dirty towels. She placed it in the cart and took a stack of clean towels inside. The final guests had checked out that morning and the Blue Moth was empty once again. Ingrid watched as Mrs. Ricci's car left the courtyard. When she turned, she saw that Norah had come back out and was watching, too.

One Sunday morning, Norah woke up early and got dressed, tying Ada's blue scarf around her hair. The girls were staying together at the Blue Moth that weekend, each with a bed to themselves since Laurel and Elena were at the bungalow. Ingrid woke up too, but didn't let on. Once Norah slipped from the room, Ingrid counted to three and then followed her. It was early October and the air was crisp and cool.

Out in the parking lot, Ingrid was surprised to see Norah climb behind the wheel of the Nissan. Laurel was driving Ada's car these days and leaving the Nissan parked at the Blue Moth. Before Norah had a chance to drive away, Ingrid hopped into the passenger seat.

What are you doing? she said.

Driving, Norah said as she turned the key.

Since when?

Elena has been teaching me, Norah said as she looked over her shoulder and reversed.

They drove in silence in the direction of the bungalow, but kept going until they reached the church. The bells were ringing when they arrived and Norah parked on the side of the road.

I'm not going in there, Ingrid said.

Do whatever you want, Norah said. She got out of the car and walked down the path towards the church. A few women standing by the door patted Norah's shoulder as she went inside.

Ingrid wandered around the cemetery during the service and sat under one of the big oak trees she and Norah used to play in. Leaning her head back against the bark, she looked up at the slivers of sky between the leaves. So far, the leaves weren't changing colour; they would start to very soon. From inside the church, the organ hummed like a giant insect. Ingrid could hear the faint sound of the choir singing, but she couldn't make out the words. She closed her eyes and listened, trying to figure out if Norah was singing too.

When she started to get cold, Ingrid stood and headed down to the beach. The service would be over soon. On the path, she stopped to remove her shoes and socks. When she straightened up again, she saw that the entire beach was covered in purple jellyfish. There was no one else around; Ingrid stared at the carnage. She had never seen so many jellyfish at once. In some places she couldn't see the sand underneath.

They get beached after the full moon, Norah said from somewhere behind her, and Ingrid jumped at the sound of her sister's voice. The High Surf warning sign was up, advising people not to swim. Each wave spewed more jellyfish onto the shore. The water was purple with jellyfish rolling against the sand. The girls started scooping them out of the waves by the armful and tossing them as far as they could, back out into the sea.

Even though they both knew the mission was futile, they kept at it for a long time. Ingrid's jeans were plastered against her legs and it felt as if she might be pulled under at any moment by the weight of them. Norah was wearing a long grey dress that looked black when it was wet. Waves broke against their shins as they tried to throw the jellyfish out far enough that the next wave wouldn't bring them back. The water was thick with the globular purple bodies, and the tendrils of their tentacles tickled Ingrid's arms. It started to rain, large drops that darkened the sand, but still they kept going.

The girls had learned in school that jellyfish are made almost entirely of water and nerve endings and absorb oxygen through their skin. But Ingrid had forgotten that they can't swim against the current. The jellyfish belonged in the ocean, but just barely; at any moment it was willing to spit them out. Ingrid also remembered learning about an immortal jellyfish in the Mediterranean that sinks to the ocean floor and regenerates. But the jellyfish on Prince Edward Island were not immortal. The water carried them along and they were powerless against the waves. The girls kept tossing them out into the water anyway, and the swells brought them back, depositing the purple bodies at their feet.

CHAPTER 19

Lewes

Julia and I continue on to Brighton to visit her parents for a couple of days. They live in a two-bedroom flat overlooking the ocean where you can always hear the waves and the seagulls squawking. It reminds me of Prince Edward Island, even though the air smells different and the beach is full of stones. When Julia and I first started seeing each other and she took me to meet her parents, I didn't know what to say or how to act. Her mom, Carla, made spaghetti and we drank chilled white wine. They asked me about my family and what Prince Edward Island was like and if I enjoyed living in Lewes. Jim, Julia's dad, made the garlic bread and the pudding. He wore an apron with a pattern of songbirds, and round glasses perched on his long nose. They were the kind of people who made you feel like you had known them forever. Julia was an only child, and it was clear her parents were proud of her. When they served tea with dessert, Jim bragged about the tea set, which Julia had made.

Carla greets us at the door.

I'm so sorry, she says to me. How are you feeling?

She's okay, mum. Julia takes my elbow. But she isn't supposed to talk much, remember?

Right, right, I'm sorry, dear, Carla says. Come on through, Jim's in the kitchen.

We follow her to the kitchen and Jim hands me a glass of ice water with lemon.

Good for the throat, he says. Their kindness nearly makes me tear up, but I hold it together and fall into the rhythm of their family conversation. We eat in the kitchen, at stools along the counter. Simple garden salads with vegetables from Carla's allotment followed by homemade flatbread pizzas. Everyone drinks lemon water. We move into the living room for tea and biscuits as Julia tells her parents about our visit to Charleston and the pub where we stayed. I let their voices wash over me as the waves of homesickness begin. When I first moved to the UK, I felt homesick all the time. Once I found the choir and Julia, the feeling subsided. But every once in a while, it sounds like there's water rushing through my ears.

I slip down the hall to the guest bedroom, where I lie on the bed and close my eyes. I roll over on my side and breathe deeply, in through the nose, out through the mouth. The door creaks open and Julia appears and sits down next to me.

Are you okay, she says. And I nod, but then I start to cry.

She lies down behind me, stroking my hair, and I curl into her as my throat tightens painfully.

I think you need to go home, Julia says. But I don't know which home she means, and my voice isn't strong enough to ask.

CHAPTER 20

Prince Edward Island, 2006 to 2007

Ingrid brought school work home for Norah and they would study together in their room at the Blue Moth, lying on their stomachs on their separate beds. Puss slept next to Norah; he rarely left her side during the weeks and months after Ada's death. Ingrid missed the little things most, like watching Ada teach Norah a new piece on the piano, helping guests with the ice machine, and answering questions about Prince Edward Island. Once, she had overheard a guest asking Elena if she was related to Anne of Green Gables, because of her red hair.

The Blue Moth Motel had survived a closure before, and Ingrid believed they could survive one again. But everything was different without Ada. Ingrid wanted to talk about her, to ask Norah what she remembered about the day the piano arrived, and to ask her about their Sunday gigs. She wanted to go back to those afternoons in the pub with people clapping.

Can we start playing at the pub again soon? Ingrid asked as she chewed on the end of her pencil. Norah was twirling her hair around her pen, creating a knot, and didn't say anything.

I think we're ready, Ingrid continued, ignoring Norah's silence. Ada would want us to.

At the sound of Ada's name, Norah sat up on the bed, threw down her pen, and left the room. Ingrid couldn't understand why no one wanted to talk about Ada. They were going through all her belongings, deciding what parts of her life were worth keeping; it was impossible for Ingrid *not* to think about her.

Ingrid groaned and flopped over onto her back. She stared up at the swirly stucco ceiling and tried not to cry. Nothing made sense anymore. She closed her eyes tight and tried to think about nothing.

Music started to drift from across the courtyard and it took Ingrid a few moments to place the melody. It was a song she had only heard once, the piece Norah wrote for Ada and performed at The Blue Moth Extravaganza. But she had changed it somehow, slowed it down so the notes sounded lonely and far away. Ingrid got up and crossed the courtyard towards the breakfast room. She stopped outside the open door, where Puss sat on guard. He stared at her with his greenish-yellow eyes, blinking slowly. Norah kept playing and Ingrid stayed outside, sitting under the window with her back against the siding, out of sight. Norah played the piece twice in a row and then the piano fell silent.

When Ingrid got up and stepped into the breakfast room, Norah was still sitting at the piano, her fingers resting lightly on the keys.

I don't want to go back to the bungalow, Norah said.

Let's stay here, then, Ingrid said.

Now every night at the Blue Moth, piano playing drifted across the empty courtyard. Norah waited until she believed Ingrid was asleep, but the music woke her up every time. She sat up in bed in the dark room and listened. Norah always played the same piece, the one she had written for Ada, but she had turned the joyful tune into something full of sadness. Then she would return to the room and put a movie in the DVD player, the volume turned low. It was often a Studio Ghibli movie, usually *When Marnie Was There*. Ingrid could tell Norah didn't want company, so she pretended to be asleep even when she could hear Norah crying.

As fall gave way to winter, Laurel and Elena stayed at the bungalow while the girls remained at the Blue Moth. The bungalow was still being cleaned out, one room at a time, and the girls hated seeing all of Ada's belongings being boxed up. Elena was the one who did most of the cleaning. She left items on the dining-room table for Laurel to go through and decide whether to keep or donate. The girls got to pick out a few things they wanted; Norah chose a couple of Ada's scarves and Ingrid took some books.

For the first time ever there was a wall between the girls. A kind of wariness. The only thing they could speak about safely was books. Mrs. Ricci continued to recommend books for Ingrid to read, and she in turn lent them to her sister. Norah figured that if she was reading, people would leave her alone.

One day in April, the girls had gone for supper at the bungalow, as they often did. A Patsy Cline record was playing in the background on Ada's old turntable, and Norah had news to share.

I got a job, she said as everyone picked up their forks. They hired me at the bookshop downtown. I start tomorrow.

Everyone fell silent except Patsy, who continued to sing about leaving. Finally, Elena spoke.

I think that's a great idea, she said. And Laurel raised her mug: A toast to Norah's new job.

I thought we were going to start singing at the pub again, Ingrid said.

You know I don't want to, Norah said. Music isn't my thing anymore.

Why are you lying? You play the piano every night!

Norah flushed but didn't say anything. With their glasses hovering, Laurel and Elena glanced back and forth between the girls.

Now you can sing whatever songs you want, Norah said. I want to do something different.

Be happy for your sister, Laurel told Ingrid as she put her glass down on the table.

But Ingrid was frightened by how far apart they all had drifted in the past ten months. It seemed like everyone had embarked on separate lives, withdrawing from each other. Elena had started night classes at the community college and Laurel was trying to figure out what to do about the Blue Moth. Everything was changing fast, and Ingrid knew she had to do something or she would be left behind.

The next morning, Ingrid found Norah standing, looking helpless, just inside the door. She was due to catch the bus for her first day at the bookshop, but she seemed frozen in place. Ingrid told her she was going to be late.

I can't do up my coat, Norah said.

She was wearing a blue zip-up raincoat with fleece inside to keep her warm.

I'll help you, Ingrid said, and she knelt down in front of her sister and coaxed the stubborn zipper back into its track. And just like that, they were kids again, getting ready to run outside and play. Cannonballs into the pool, hide and seek in the cemetery, performing at the pub. But when Ingrid stood up, they were teenagers again, being forced to figure out which type of world they wanted to live in.

Thanks, Norah said as she picked up her bag. See you tonight.

Ingrid went to the bookshop after school and wandered the aisles until Norah's shift was over. She watched her restocking the shelves, recommending books to customers, and placing their purchases in crinkly paper bags. Norah was wearing a long wool skirt and stockings and had pulled her blond hair into a bun at the base of her neck. A few months shy of her sixteenth birthday, Norah was still shorter than Ingrid. But right now she did look like the older sister.

Publishers sent free books and advance reading copies which Norah was allowed to take home. She shared them with Ingrid and they talked about the characters like they were real people. It was easier to talk about fictional worlds than the real one. As summer approached and the whole island seemed to come to life, the lingering question was whether the Blue Moth would reopen. Laurel hadn't decided yet, though she had arranged to fill the pool up, even if just for the girls. The washers and dryers which used to run daily now only ran once or twice a week— Ingrid even missed the smell of dryer sheets which used to float on the air. The courtyard was an independent ecosystem, but without any guests, Ingrid felt like she and Norah were going extinct.

In June, Sophie called and invited the girls to visit her for a week in Nova Scotia. Laurel and Elena agreed that it would be nice for them to go somewhere on their own. So, soon after school let out for the summer, Ingrid and Norah boarded the bus which travelled between the three Maritime provinces. The bus picked them up at the university. And Ingrid thought of how she couldn't wait to go to university herself, to walk along a tree-lined path between old brick buildings. She was determined to get a scholarship for a music program, but she wasn't sure where. All she knew was that home felt claustrophobic and stationary and she wanted to escape.

The girls sat at the back of the bus and Norah waved out the window to Laurel and Elena. Ingrid put their backpacks in the overhead bin. It was almost the one-year anniversary of Ada's passing, but no one had said a word about it and the girls would be in Nova Scotia on the exact date. Ingrid wondered if Laurel had agreed to the trip because of its timing. Without Norah and her around, Laurel would be free to grieve in peace.

Sophie and her mom met them at the bus station and the three girls piled into the back seat of the car. They had to be reminded to put their seat belts on because they were talking so fast. It was easy to forget about everything when they were around Sophie, who was telling them about all the things she had planned for the week. She said she lived close to the harbour, downtown stores, and a big park, so they would have lots of places to explore. When they arrived, Ingrid stared up at the three-storey home with its front-porch swing and gabled windows. Sophie's dad was a doctor and her mom taught biology at the nearby university. Ingrid had never known someone who lived in a house like this. It was the type of home she dreamed of living in one day, but she had no idea how to make that happen.

They carried their backpacks up the steps and Sophie led them through the front door into an entryway with high ceilings and a curved staircase. Everything was painted white and gleaming. It smelled as if someone had just washed the floors. The girls followed Sophie into the kitchen, where they sat at an island and ate crackers topped with chunky peanut butter. Sophie's dad was working the night shift, so he had to sleep all day. When they were in the house, they had to be quiet, but Sophie didn't think they would be spending much time inside.

The guest room was painted pale blue and had a king-sized bed covered with a thick white duvet and plump white pillows. It reminded Ingrid of the bed at Arabella by the Sea; she wanted to curl up under the covers. Then Sophie showed them her room, which was painted dark green. The wall behind her bed was covered with pictures cut out of magazines—palm trees and swimming pools and Italian cafes. An antique desk and chair sat under the window, which overlooked the backyard. There was a tidy bookshelf and a pile of laundry in the corner. Sophie sat down on her bed and rummaged in the drawer of her bedside table.

Here it is! she said after a minute, holding up a crumpled twenty-dollar bill.

Sophie told her mom where they were going, and the three girls left the house, tiptoeing down the steps. Sophie led the way to her favourite coffee shop. She ordered for Ingrid and Norah too, three lattes, and they took their treat down to the harbour where they sat on a bench overlooking the water. The noise and bustle of Halifax was like waking up after a year of hibernation. There was a man unloading two mannequins from the trunk of his car and one of the plastic heads fell off and rolled down the hill towards the harbour. Two dogs barked at each other from opposite sides of the street and their owners held them back.

When Sophie asked what the girls had been up to for the past year, Ingrid couldn't think of anything to tell her. Norah talked about her job at the bookshop and Puss. Neither of them mentioned music or Ada. They had messaged Sophie about these things, a little bit, but they didn't know how to talk about them face to face.

They walked back to Sophie's house and bounced on the

trampoline in her back yard. When they were tired, they lay down in the centre and stared up at the sky. Part of the house was visible and it looked even bigger upside down. Ingrid wondered what it must have been like to grow up in a house like that, if she would have been a different person if she had lived Sophie's life.

The week with Sophie was the happiest time the girls had had all year. They went for walks in the park, sat under trees near the waterfront, and watched movies on a big screen TV. On Friday night, Sophie said some of her friends from school were having a party and they were invited. But Norah didn't want to go. She said they hadn't brought anything to wear to a party.

Okay, Sophie said. We don't have to go. I have another idea.

Sophie's dad was working and her mom was spending the evening with friends, so they had the house to themselves. Downstairs, Sophie grabbed a bottle of red wine from the rack and three juice glasses. They took blankets and pillows to the trampoline to sleep there. It was a warm night for late June, but they wore hoodies and thick socks to keep out the damp. They arranged their blankets and pillows in a circle and Sophie poured the wine. It was the first time the girls had tasted wine, but they tried to pretend it wasn't. They took turns telling ghost stories as the dusk faded to darkness and they could only see the outline of each other.

It's one year today, Norah said.

To Ada, Ingrid said, raising her wine glass.

The girls drank and Ingrid wiped her mouth with the back of her hand. It was as if the trampoline had disappeared from beneath them and they were floating in mid-air in their blankets. Even though Ingrid didn't really like the taste of the wine, she liked how it made her mind fuzzy and her body warm.

Let's play Never Have I Ever, Sophie said as she refilled their glasses. I'll go first. Never have I ever peed outside.

Ingrid thought of all those summer afternoons in the cemetery when she and Norah had squatted behind trees or run down into the ocean.

I really haven't! Sophie said.

Do it now, then, Norah said. Go behind one of those trees.

Sophie jumped down from the trampoline, and a motion sensor light came on and illuminated part of the back yard. Ingrid shielded her eyes from the light, which made her feel like she was on a stage. She and Norah watched as Sophie stumbled over to a tree and disappeared behind it. They heard the zipper of her jeans and the swoosh of fabric. Then nothing for a few moments. Finally, Sophie reappeared and raised her arms in the air.

Done, she said, and the girls clapped.

A few minutes after Sophie was settled on the trampoline again, the light went off.

Okay, your turn, Ingrid, Sophie said.

Never have I ever kissed anyone, Ingrid said. As soon as the words were out, her face flushed, and she was grateful for the darkness. Going into high school, Ingrid still didn't know some things that she was sure everyone else had a grasp of. Towards the end of Grade Nine, a lot of kids had paired up and talked about going on dates to the movie theatre and coffee shops. In some of the books she read, girls her age had summer romances that seemed glamorous. But Ingrid didn't know how to ask Laurel about anything like that. She wanted to ask how Laurel knew she loved Elena and if she had loved their dad.

Norah took a glug of wine. Me neither, she said. And I don't think I want to yet.

That's okay, Sophie said.

I want to, Ingrid said. Do you love Tom?

Sophie paused for a second. I think so. It's complicated.

They fell silent and listened to the crickets chirping. Ingrid raised her glass of wine.

I think, Ingrid said, speaking slowly, I think I would rather kiss girls than boys.

Norah hiccupped and leaned her head against Ingrid's shoulder.

It's okay if you don't know for sure, Sophie said. Sometimes it takes a while.

Okay, Norah, your turn, Ingrid said, eager to change the subject. She nudged her sister with her elbow.

Never have I ever, Norah said, sang a song entirely on my own.

Sing for us now, Ingrid said. It's too dark for us to see you anyway, so you can pretend you're alone.

We'll be really quiet, Sophie said.

Norah inhaled deeply, as if getting ready to dive underwater. As she began to sing, her voice was soft and reedy. She sang one of their oldest pieces, Dolly Parton's original version of "I Will Always Love You," and as she kept going her voice strengthened. When she reached the chorus for the second time, Ingrid joined in softly, slotting her voice into harmony. It had been so long since Ingrid heard Norah sing that she was surprised at how clear and true her sister's voice sounded.

When the song ended, Sophie clapped. I don't know what I was expecting, she said. But it wasn't that.

≡≡≡≡≡

Norah decided to return to school for Grade Ten. So the girls set out together for the big regional high school. They were pretty alone once they arrived, though. Kids from different middle schools filtered into the school, so in each class of thirty or so kids, they recognized only a handful. And gym was one of the only classes they were in together.

One day in the locker room before gym class, a girl named Kate pointed at Ingrid's bare legs and said, loudly, You don't shave yet? Norah, who'd been getting changed in a bathroom stall, had just emerged with her clothes draped over her arm. She looked at Kate. So? she said quietly, I don't shave either.

Ingrid wasn't sure whether Norah thought this bit of information would be helpful, but it just made Kate laugh and some of the other girls joined in. Ingrid was proud of her sister, though, whose face was now turning red as she shoved her clothes into her gym bag.

Your *moms* probably don't shave either, Kate said.

Ingrid stepped forward towards Kate, who was smiling now, hands on her hips. It wasn't so much what Kate had said, but how she said it, the emphasis she placed on the word. This was the same Kate from middle school, Kate of the butterfly-tattoo rumour. Ingrid was thinking about this as she stepped right up to Kate and punched her perfect little nose.

Kate screamed, and the sound echoed off the tiled walls like the call of a fox. Her friends surrounded her as she fell back dramatically onto one of the benches, holding her hands to her face and glaring at Ingrid through bloodied fingers. Ingrid's ears started ringing and it felt like she was floating above everyone else, looking down on a scene she had nothing to do with. Norah grabbed her arm and started to steer her out of the room. Behind them, Kate's screams faded into soft wailing.

At that moment the gym teacher, Ms. Smith, threw open the locker room door.

What's going on here? Ms. Smith said. When she saw Norah's pale face and Ingrid's wild eyes, she put her hand up on the door frame to prevent them from leaving.

My office, she said. Both of you.

Ms. Smith continued into the locker room to check on Kate. Norah had a tight grip on Ingrid's elbow, and she led her sister to Ms. Smith's office. They sat on a pile of blue plastic gym mats which were stacked in the corner. The room smelled like plastic water bottles, sweat, and old microwave dinners. On the desk, there was a picture of a young girl crouched next to a German shepherd on a path in the woods. The girl was smiling, her arm draped over the dog's back, and dappled sunlight fell through the trees onto the path.

Norah took Ingrid's hands and turned them over. There was dried blood on her knuckles and a slight bruise rising. Ingrid didn't realize she was crying until Norah grabbed a box of tissues from the desk and held them out. Ms. Smith appeared a few minutes later and closed her office door. She went over to the mini-fridge beside her desk and removed an ice pack, which she wrapped in a thin towel and placed over Ingrid's knuckles. Leaning back on her heels in front of the girls, she sighed.

I know Kate is a bully, Ms. Smith said. And that isn't right. But retaliating in this way isn't right either, Ingrid, and I know you know that.

Ingrid nodded and stared down at her hand. It was throbbing, and the ice pack made it feel a little bit better.

She got suspended for two weeks. Any time there was blood involved, it was difficult to make the principal understand the real details of the story. The one bleeding was the victim and the one with the bruised knuckles was at fault. Ingrid sat in a chair across from the principal's desk while he explained everything to her. Ms. Smith hovered by the door, her arms crossed over her chest, and Ingrid glanced back at her once or twice. There was something in the gym teacher's face that made Ingrid think she didn't completely agree with the principal's decision, but it wasn't her place to say otherwise.

When Laurel arrived at the school, she walked through the main door with knitted brows. Ingrid sat waiting on a bench outside the office with the ice pack still wrapped around her hand, but it had melted and the water sloshed back and forth when she moved. Laurel went into the office to speak with the principal, and when she came back out she looked angrier than before. Leaving the melted ice pack on the bench, Ingrid followed her mother out to the car. Neither of them said a word as they climbed in. Ingrid leaned forward to turn the radio on, but Laurel clicked it off, shaking her head as they drove away from the school. Expecting a lecture, Ingrid leaned back in her seat, but Laurel remained silent. Ingrid resisted the desire to ask where they were going.

The two of them rarely spent time together on their own. Ingrid tried to remember a time but couldn't. Norah was always there, or Elena. As Laurel drove, she gripped the steering wheel tightly with both hands and leaned forward so her back didn't touch the seat. Ingrid couldn't figure out if Laurel was mad at her or at something else.

Laurel parked by the water, at the end of a long boardwalk where people ran and walked their dogs. She turned off the car but kept her hands on the steering wheel and stared straight out at the water.

People are always going to judge you for the way you live, Laurel said. And sometimes they'll judge you for who you love, as well. People don't like things they don't understand. But you're very lucky. You know why?

Ingrid shook her head. She stared at Laurel's profile, her sharp nose and chin, and realized she was still wearing her uniform from the restaurant. She looked tired, somehow, and older than she was.

Because you have two parents who love you very much and also love each other, Laurel continued. She finally turned and looked at Ingrid. I'm not sure if your classmate Kate can say the same about her family.

Oh, Ingrid said.

You have to think about where other people are coming from, Laurel said. And use your voice instead, okay?

They got out of the car and started walking along the board-walk.

Do you and Elena want to get married? Ingrid asked.

I don't know, Laurel said. Maybe someday. Now that we're allowed.

≡≡≡

At the end of September, the pool was scheduled to be emptied for the season. On the final day, Ingrid sat in a lawn chair all morning. She was still suspended and the days seemed endless. Books and music only distracted her for so long and she spent most of the time staring up at the plastic palm trees or trailing a piece of ribbon across the ground for Puss to chase. He didn't like Ingrid as much as Norah, but when Norah wasn't around he tolerated her presence.

Around lunchtime, Ingrid decided to walk into the city and wait for Norah outside the school. She was hungry when she arrived and she realized she hadn't brought any money. The bell rang, signalling lunch, and Ingrid watched from the other side of the parking lot as teenagers poured out through the doors and jumped into their cars to go get fast food. Radios blared as the cars and trucks peeled out of the parking lot, each boy trying to squeal his tires louder than the one in front of him. Ingrid knew Norah would be in the courtyard outside the library, so she walked around the perimeter of the school, staying close to the trees so no one would notice her.

Norah did a double take when she saw her sister. Ingrid sat down across from her at the picnic table and took half of her egg salad sandwich. They were the only ones in the courtyard other than the songbirds who were hopping around on the pavement, waiting for crumbs. Norah took a bag of sunflower seeds out of her backpack and scattered some on the ground. As the girls shared apple slices and cubes of cheese, they watched the birds hopping and flapping their wings.

Meet me at the pharmacy after school, Norah said when the bell rang. Ingrid nodded and remained at the picnic table for a few minutes after Norah disappeared inside. Two whole hours to fill before school was out for the day, so Ingrid decided to walk around the city and look at the historical houses. She made up stories about the people who lived in them, their jobs, what they ate for breakfast, even their names.

There was one large house with green siding and a wrap-around porch which had a baby grand piano in a room that overlooked the street. No one was playing it, so Ingrid stood and stared in through the window. Sunshine glinted on the black surface of the piano and a few photographs in silver frames sat on the closed top. Norah would love to play a piano like that, and Ingrid pictured her sister sitting in front of the instrument, playing loudly with the windows open for the entire city to hear.

Ingrid kept walking, stopping every now and then to glance into a window or pet a passing cat. She picked up a fallen maple leaf and twirled it between her fingers, watching as it blurred into a solid colour. Ingrid walked to the pharmacy and sat on the bench outside to wait for Norah. A little ways down the street, a man stood in a doorway in a cowboy hat, playing guitar and singing a country song. Beside him, his guitar case lay open on the sidewalk. His voice echoed down the street, twangy and slightly off key, but Ingrid admired him.

Shortly after three o'clock, Norah appeared with her backpack and a plastic bag full of homework for Ingrid, who stood up and followed Norah into the store. An employee who was stocking shelves looked them up and down—any teenager with a backpack was automatically suspicious—but decided they were harmless and returned to restocking the magazines. Ingrid followed Norah down one of the aisles, unsure of their mission. Norah stopped at the shaving section and chose a package of pink disposable razors and a purple aerosol can of shaving gel, which she handed to Ingrid. At the checkout, Norah grabbed a package of gum and a chocolate bar as well and paid with her debit card. The cashier put everything in a plastic bag and the girls left the pharmacy to start their walk home.

As they crossed the Hillsborough bridge, they shared the chocolate bar, passing it back and forth. Ingrid carried her bag of homework and Norah carried the gel and razors. At the Blue Moth, the girls changed into their bathing suits. The crisp air made goosebumps rise on their arms and legs as they crossed the courtyard to the pool, Norah still carrying the plastic bag. They sat side by side on the edge and dangled their legs in the water. Norah took the shaving cream and razors out of the bag and told Ingrid to hold out her hand so she could squeeze some of the gel onto her palm. It expanded into foam.

Rub it on your leg and then I'll show you how to use the razor, Norah said.

I wish Sophie was here, Ingrid said as she lifted one of her legs out of the water and did as Norah instructed. The foam smelled like sugary chemicals. Norah slid the little blade guard off one of the razors and held it out.

Go against the hair, she said. And don't press too hard.

Ingrid nodded and slowly moved the razor up her leg. The smooth, hairless skin revealed underneath the foam was clean and brand new. It looked like her leg belonged to someone else. The paths through the shaving foam reminded Ingrid of when Ada mowed the lawn around the Blue Moth and left neat stripes in the grass.

Norah started on her own legs, and when both girls were finished shaving they wiped the foam off with a towel and jumped into the pool. The water felt colder than usual against their legs and they shrieked. Ingrid ducked under and swam all the way to the bottom, where a pile of leaves and sand swirled in a circle. Norah swam down too, and they sat cross-legged with their eyes open, blowing streams of bubbles out through their noses.

When they surfaced, the service people were there to drain the water and secure the winter tarp. Reluctantly, the girls climbed out and headed to their room. Once they were dressed and had towels wrapped around their wet hair, they sat in the plastic chairs outside their door. They watched as the pool water drained away and took summer with it.

CHAPTER 21

Lewes

The weather is finally warm enough for me to swim at the Pells Pool. I wake early, at the same time as Julia, and we have breakfast together before going our separate ways. She kisses me goodbye on the street in front of her apartment. A few other lane swimmers are already in the water when I arrive. The pool is fed by a natural spring, so the water often feels crisp at the beginning of the season but warms up as summer progresses. There's a canteen that sells ice cream, but it isn't open in the mornings. I get changed, leave my clothes in a locker, and head out to the deck. The water shimmers in the sun and I sit on the edge and dangle my feet in. If I really try, I can pretend I'm back at the Blue Moth with Norah on a hot summer afternoon. I miss the plastic palm trees and the smell of seaweed and Norah's voice. I put my goggles on and slip under the water.

I swim laps and then lay on my towel in the grass. There are people leaning against the trees and kids kicking a ball around. The sky is pale blue, no clouds, and I wonder what the weather is like on Prince Edward Island. It feels like I exist in two places simultaneously. I close my eyes, my limbs heavy from swimming, and listen to the birds singing in the trees. Something bumps against my shoulder and I open my eyes, shading them from the sun with my arm. It's a red ball with a smile painted on it. A girl comes running over to retrieve it.

Sorry, she says as I toss her the ball. My brother doesn't have very good aim. She's wearing a denim dress and has short, dark hair cut in a bob. I smile in what I hope is a reassuring way, and she hovers, looking at my towel, which has music notes on it. They're a random pattern, not any particular song, but the girl is trying to read them anyway. I pick up my phone, type out a message, and hand it to her.

Oh, she says. I'm sorry about your voice.

She sits down in the grass next to me and begins to pick dandelions and braid them together.

I like singing too, she says. And playing the violin. But I'm only allowed to do that at school because my dad says it makes too much noise.

I type her another message and we continue our conversation like this for a little while. It's the longest conversation I've had with someone other than Julia or Susan. When her brother finally comes over to take the ball, the girl stands and places the dandelion crown on my head before she skips off to continue her game.

I stay on the grass until the place starts to get busier, then I pack up and walk back to Julia's. On my way, I stop at a flower shop and purchase a bouquet of purple tulips. They haven't opened yet, and I put them in one of Julia's vases on the kitchen table so they're the first thing she'll see when she gets home.

CHAPTER 22

Prince Edward Island, 2007 to 2008

After school on Mondays, Wednesdays, and Fridays, Norah went to work at the bookshop while Ingrid explored downtown. One afternoon, Ingrid stood watching the country singer on the sidewalk. He tipped his cowboy hat whenever someone tossed change into his guitar case. He was always there, she realized. Every time she came downtown. And now she remembered that she'd seen him once before: that day after she and Norah had their first gig in the pub.

In the bookshop, Norah was dusting books with a blue feather duster. Ingrid followed her around the store as she worked, talking about the man.

You should try it, Norah said.

But I don't know how to play guitar, Ingrid said.

Just sing, you don't need any other instrument.

Mom won't like it.

Norah stopped dusting for a moment and turned to look at her sister. Don't tell her, then, she said.

Will you sing with me? Ingrid asked.

Norah shook her head. You don't need me, she said. She continued dusting and moved farther down the row of books.

As Ingrid left the bookshop, she thought about all the money she could earn, and how she could save it and use it to travel and to swim in all those oceans they had dreamed of. She wanted to figure out who she was outside the courtyard of the Blue Moth Motel.

The next day after school, Ingrid stood next to a bench on a cobblestone street lined with restaurants and gift shops. She placed a Mason jar by her feet and started to sing. There weren't many tourists around, since it was coming to the end of the season, but a few people stopped to listen. Every time someone tossed some change into the jar, Ingrid nodded her head in thanks and kept singing.

When Norah's shift was over, she went to find her sister. Ingrid had made ten dollars in just over an hour and the girls went to a nearby cafe and sat at a table by the window. Looking around, Ingrid saw university students typing away on laptops, business people having meetings, and tourists admiring the historical atmosphere of the cafe, with its exposed brick walls. The hiss of the steam wand and the hum of people's voices added an undercurrent to the soft jazz music playing on the speakers. Ingrid bought two cappuccinos. She watched the barista steam the milk and pour it in a neat swirling motion into the white cups. The barista made a fern design with the milk and placed each cup carefully in its saucer. These were the first cappuccinos the girls had ever tasted, and they took their first sips in unison, smiling at each other over the top of their cups. The foamy milk was soft and sweet. Even though Ingrid was too young to drink caffeine, according to Lauren, the taste of coffee reminded her of the camping trip to Nova Scotia. But the cappuccino tasted much better.

The girls fell into a quiet routine for the rest of the fall and the winter. Three days a week, Ingrid sang outside the coffee shop until Norah finished work, then they met up and took turns buying each other cappuccinos. Singing in the winter was challenging; Ingrid wrapped a scarf tightly around her neck and wore mittens with hand warmers inside. There were fewer people on the streets, but they often gave more money because of the cold. Stepping inside the warm cafe after singing in the cold quickly became one of Ingrid's favourite things. With pink cheeks and cold toes, she counted her money and tucked it away. Norah brought books from the store and they read into the evening. Ingrid still carried the copy of *The Waves* which Mrs. Ricci had given her. Even though she had read it three times, she still didn't understand it. But she loved how the words flowed, and someday she would figure out the meaning. Lingering at their table by the window meant the girls spent less time at the Blue Moth, which was starting to feel like a haunted house. All those empty rooms stood gathering dust while Laurel and Elena tried to figure out what to do with it.

In the spring, everything started to wake up again. Tourists returned, but the Blue Moth remained closed. One afternoon, when Ingrid was singing outside the coffee shop, Mrs. Ricci appeared and stopped to listen. She held a bag from the bookshop and was wearing a long tan trench coat that made her look like she was visiting from a different decade. When Ingrid finished her song, Mrs. Ricci stepped forward and handed her a five dollar bill.

You should be in the school choir, she said.

Ingrid took a sip from her water bottle and thanked her. But I don't think I'd fit in.

I don't think you would either, Mrs. Ricci said. That's the whole point.

⎯⎯⎯

Mrs. Ricci let Ingrid join the choir for the remaining three months of Grade Ten. The choir met before school on Tuesdays and Thursdays, so Norah drove Ingrid to school early. The Nissan had started to retain the odour of deep-fried food from the roadside restaurant, which seeped into Laurel and Elena's uniforms and refused to fade, no matter how many times they washed them. So Norah asked if she could drive Ada's Cadillac, and Laurel said yes.

Ingrid tried to convince Norah to join the choir too, but she refused. Ingrid argued that Norah's voice would blend in with the others, so no one would hear her anyway. But Norah stuck with her decision.

I don't love music as much as I did when we were kids, Norah said. I know you still do, but it's different for me.

Yet every night, Norah still snuck out to the breakfast room and played the piano when she thought no one was listening. It was as if she had decided that the musical part of her life was over and she wanted to be someone new, but she couldn't let go completely.

In choir, Ingrid felt left behind. Everyone was nice to her and tried to make sure she felt included. But the others had been singing together since the fall—since those early weeks of high school when Grade Ten students try to find their people. Ingrid realized this now, too late. Some had joined the band or choir, while others went out for drama club. There was an art group that met during lunch hour and a yearbook committee that hung out in one of the computer labs. The groups you joined let everyone know what type of person you were. And by not joining any of them, Ingrid had become invisible.

The other singers were also more advanced musically. Along with her academic homework, Ingrid practised sight-reading and all the vocal exercises Mrs. Ricci assigned them. She shut herself in the bathroom at the Blue Moth, where her voice bounced off the tiles and sounded more full. By being in the choir, Ingrid realized that Ada had taught them a lot but not nearly enough. Their pub and church gigs had been the perfect introduction, but Ingrid wanted to keep improving and learning. Singing was going to be her way out.

One of the tenors, George, was very kind to Ingrid and helped her with her sight-reading. Sometimes they met up in the choir room at recess and lunch to practise. George was tall, lanky, and awkward; he often knocked over the music stand with his knees when he sat down. But his voice was deep and strong. Another latecomer had joined the choir that term: Kate. Towards the end of the school year, she started turning up too, to do her homework. She would sit at a desk in the corner, shoulders hunched over her paper, rarely looking up. Ingrid and George sat on the opposite side of the room and they started to feel awkward for not including Kate. She had braces now, and seemed to spend a lot of time alone. Her gaggle of giggling friends spent their lunch hours in the smoking section or leaning up against trucks in the parking lot. Kate used to be their leader, Ingrid thought. Clearly not anymore.

Every year, the school had an end-of-year Fun Fair with cotton candy machines, face painting, and clowns wandering around on stilts. Everyone made fun of the event and said it was juvenile, but then they'd go—and have a blast. There was a dunk tank, a bake sale, and a slip-n-slide on the hill by the soccer field. A long blue tarp had been slathered in dish soap and the boys from the soccer team had run a hose out from the gym to keep it slippery. People took turns sliding down the hill, some wearing bathing suits and some still in their clothes. Ingrid, Norah, and George sat together in the grass eating bright pink cotton candy. They watched their more athletic classmates take running leaps and cringed for them as they slid on their stomachs down the tarp. A few of the Grade Twelve girls had fake tans in preparation for prom and their skin looked orange in the early summer sun.

The cotton candy made Ingrid's teeth hurt, so she set the rest of hers down in the grass and watched as ants appeared and swarmed the pink sugar. People on the hill started cheering and whooping, so Ingrid looked up and saw Kate at the top of the slip-n-slide. She was taking off her clothes and one of the boys from the soccer team whistled but she ignored him. She wasn't wearing a bathing suit but had on plain black underwear and a sports bra. Leaving her clothes in a pile at the top of the hill, Kate ran towards the tarp and flew down it on her feet like she was surfing. When she reached the bottom of the hill, everyone cheered. Kate walked back up the hill and collected her clothes, but rather than putting them back on right away, she bunched them up under her arm and headed straight towards Ingrid, Norah, and George. She stopped in front of them, close enough for Ingrid to see the pieces of grass stuck to her calves. Unlike everyone else who had gone down the slip-n-slide, Kate was dry except for her legs.

I'm sorry, she said. About . . . you know.

I know, Ingrid said. Me too.

Kate stuck out her hand. Truce?

Ingrid thought for a moment. She looked up at Kate and reached up and took her hand.

And just like that, Ingrid had another friend. If she had realized it was so easy to talk to people, she would have tried to make friends sooner. Sophie, in Halifax, was headed for university, drifting away, and Kate quickly stepped into the gap.

Kate lived in a trailer park behind the shopping mall. Ingrid learned that Kate's parents had divorced at the end of Grade Nine and she and her mom had moved into the trailer. Her dad had a new girlfriend, and he lived with her in in the historical downtown house where they used to live as a family. Kate spent the weekends there, but she stayed in her room with the door closed and practised her singing so she wouldn't have to talk to them.

On the days when Ingrid wasn't singing downtown, she went to Kate's and they sat on the sofa and ate crackers with peanut butter. The trailer looked more like a bungalow than a house on wheels. It had two bedrooms, one at either end. Kate said there were a few other people from school who lived in the park, but she wasn't friends with any of them. They stood at the bus stop together every morning but they were all in their own private worlds. Ingrid liked how people in the trailer park decorated their lawns with garden gnomes and plants in ceramic pots. People talked to each other over fences and waved when they walked by with their dogs.

One day in June, George stood at the front of the room before early-morning choir practice began and asked everyone to be quiet.

It's Kate's birthday today, he announced. When she comes in, let's sing "Happy Birthday" for her.

Everyone agreed and took their seats, arranging sheet music and pretending to be busy. When Kate walked in a few minutes later, George acted as conductor and gave them the signal to start singing. People exaggerated their voices, singing loud and in a silly tone. Kate stood just inside the door and covered her face with her hands. When the song finished, she clapped, her face flushed and smiling, and took her place next to Ingrid as Mrs. Ricci arrived.

Okay, everyone! Mrs. Ricci said, shooing George back to his seat. Time to get to work.

By the time the end-of-year performance came around, the choir had become like Ingrid's second family, especially Kate and George. The three of them spent all their free time together. Sometimes Norah joined them but since she wasn't in the choir she missed out on some of the inside jokes about the haughtiness of the tech crew and the specific way Mrs. Ricci clapped her hands, which always made at least one person jump. Ingrid knew her sister felt left out, but she didn't know how to fix it. Norah would eat lunch with them and then slip away to the library while Kate, George, and Ingrid went to one of the computer labs to watch videos. Even though YouTube was blocked, George knew how to get around it. All they wanted to watch was other school choirs, to hear the songs they were singing and learn from them.

One lunch hour, they stumbled across a video of a Julie Andrews concert from 1993. Ingrid clicked on it so fast George didn't have time to protest. The concert was in Tokyo and the three of them watched Andrews step onto the stage in a shiny gold ball gown, to thunderous applause. The full orchestra behind her played "The Sound of Music" as she stretched out her arms and did her signature twirl from the movie. Then she began to sing. The three of them sat riveted as her voice filled the small computer room, and Ingrid fumbled with the volume, hoping they hadn't attracted the attention of any teacher in a nearby classroom. The three of them leaned closer to the screen. The ball gown looked like it was made out of gold leaf. It had puffed sleeves and shimmered under the lights as Julie Andrews moved across the stage. Halfway through the video she had a wardrobe change, reappearing in a black velvet dress with a drop waist and white tulle at the shoulders. She was so elegant, her voice soaring over the orchestra. Ingrid wanted to be just like her. But Ingrid knew her voice wasn't like Julie Andrews'; as Ingrid got older, her voice had deepened, and she had resigned herself to her place as an alto.

The performance was nearly an hour long, so the bell rang signalling the end of lunch long before it was over. Ingrid groaned as George closed the browser and they gathered up their things and made their way to class. But Ingrid couldn't stop thinking about the concert. When she got to the Blue Moth later, she watched the entire thing on the computer in the office.

Kate loved the Blue Moth and wanted to swim in the pool. Laurel agreed to have it filled for the season, as long as Ingrid would keep it clean. Since she didn't have an official job other than busking, Ingrid agreed. She got up early every morning and went out to the courtyard. She unwound the long blue pool vacuum tube and attached the nozzle. The blue pool cover looked like a big sheet of bubble wrap. Ingrid gathered it up and shoved it into the Rubbermaid bin where it was kept during the day. She put the vacuum in the water and began to clean. The water distorted the handle and made it look like it was broken. Methodically, she cleaned up all the leaves and sand.

One morning, Norah and Puss were in the breakfast room when Ingrid walked in after doing the pool. Norah had a bowl of cereal on the table in front of her and was eating it slowly while Puss watched as if he was supervising. Ingrid made toast and joined her sister.

Norah had started working full-time as soon as school let out, and she'd be leaving in a minute to catch the bus. When school started up again in September, she'd go back down to part-time. She kept trying to convince Ingrid to get a real job, but the flexibility of busking suited Ingrid more.

Are you going to sing this afternoon? Norah asked.

Maybe, Ingrid said. As long as it doesn't rain.

Okay, Norah said as she stood up. See you later, then.

As Norah gathered up her bag and made to leave, Puss trotted along behind her. She stopped and turned in the doorway to face Ingrid again.

I miss her, Norah said.

I know, Ingrid said. Me too.

―――――――――

The Blue Moth was quiet, too quiet, so Ingrid would call Kate. If it wasn't raining, they swam, and on rainy days Kate picked Ingrid up in her mother's truck and they drove around. They drove the coastal route and sang along with the radio. One day in late August, it was threatening rain, so they decided to go for an adventure. As Kate merged onto the highway, Ingrid reached forward and turned the radio down.

What happened with your old friends? she asked.

Kate sighed, her hands gripping the steering wheel. They didn't think I was interesting anymore, she said. I got braces, my parents divorced.

I like your braces, Ingrid said.

And I guess I realized making fun of people makes me feel crappy, Kate continued. She glanced quickly at Ingrid before returning her gaze to the road.

I like everyone in the choir, Kate said. I wasted so much time trying to fit in with the wrong people while all of you were having fun.

Ingrid thought of all the lunch hours spent fundraising for the choir to attend regional competitions, selling baked goods and gift-basket tickets from a table set up in the cafeteria. Sometimes the boys from the soccer team threw french fries at the table. Loaded with ketchup, they landed with a splat.

Ingrid reached forward and turned the radio up again. A song by Cher came on, and they sang along. A few songs later, Kate exited the highway and turned down an old road full of potholes. She drove slowly, avoiding most of them, and Ingrid leaned forward in her seat to see where they were going. Up ahead, the gates of Fairyland loomed on the side of the road and Kate turned into the parking lot, which was overgrown with weeds. Fairyland was an old amusement park that had been shut down years earlier. Laurel and Elena had never taken the girls there because the tickets were too expensive. But they'd driven by many times and Ingrid had begged to go in.

Welcome to Scaryland, Kate said. She parked the truck in a grove of trees so it couldn't be seen from the road and they got out. There was a No Trespassing sign hanging from a length of chain across the entrance, but it was hardly enough to keep anyone out. Graffiti tags covered the walls and beer cans littered the ground.

The air was humid, still threatening rain. Ingrid half-expected to see a guard in one of the ticket booths, waiting to catch trespassers, but both booths were empty. Kate stepped over the chain and Ingrid followed.

Did you come here as a kid? Ingrid asked as they entered the main area of the park. The wave pool was empty and covered in graffiti. All the snack booths were boarded up.

Yeah, sometimes, Kate said. I liked to ride the train but I never wanted to get off. I was content to just ride around in circles all day through the woods. Did you come here?

Ingrid shook her head.

Come on, Kate said, taking Ingrid's hand. Let's go find the train.

They left the main area and headed towards the woods. The station remained, but the train cars were long gone. Ingrid knew that the tracks went through the woods, past little houses where characters from fairy tales lived in a kid-sized version of Cinderella's castle, Snow White's cottage, and Sleeping Beauty's tower room. She remembered hearing stories from her classmates about playing in the wave pool and eating hot pretzels on the train. The wooden tracks were rotting away; weeds and ivy grew around the wood and tried to reclaim it as part of the forest. Other trespassers had carved their names and initials into the railings, scratching off the peeling paint. Kate stepped gingerly onto the train platform, testing the strength of the wood. She picked up a rock and started carving.

This is creepy, Ingrid said. We should go before it rains.

Not yet, Kate said. We have to see the houses.

They followed the train tracks deeper into the woods, the pine trees creaking around them. Snow White's cottage appeared. There was a wooden sign next to a path which led to a small front door, just big enough for an eight-year-old to fit through without ducking. The cottage was slowly being absorbed back into nature, but the sloping roof still stood strong. Kate strode up to the door and pulled some weeds aside so she could shove it open. She ducked her head and stepped in; Ingrid followed, not wanting to be left alone.

The heavy smell of must filled their noses and Ingrid had the sensation of being watched. It was dim inside the cottage, but as her eyes adjusted, Ingrid gasped and grabbed Kate's arm. They were surrounded by the seven dwarves, their clothes faded and covered with dust, their beards yellowed with age. Their faces were happy, hands raised as if they were waving hello. A table was set for tea, the cups full of dead flies, and in the middle of the room Snow White lay in her glass coffin in a white nightgown, surrounded by faded plastic flowers. The mannequin was about the height of a ten-year-old and her hands were folded and resting on her chest, holding a bouquet.

Holy shit, Ingrid said. This is a nightmare. She turned to leave, but Kate stopped her.

Stay just for a second, Kate said.

Ingrid imagined dust settling in her lungs, but she stayed. Kate let go of Ingrid's arm and stepped towards Snow White. Ingrid tried not to think about dust accumulating in the rooms at the Blue Moth, how someday it might end up like Fairyland with trees growing through the floors and wallpaper peeling off in sheets. A greyish light was falling through the small windows of the cottage and Ingrid watched as Kate's shoes left prints in the dust-coated floor. Barely breathing, Ingrid watched Kate approach the coffin. She lifted the hem of her T-shirt and wiped the glass.

There, Kate said. Now she can see everything.

CHAPTER 23

Lewes

My bank balance gets dangerously low. One morning, after Julia leaves for work, I book a plane ticket with my credit card. When I receive the confirmation email, I close my laptop and get out of bed. By now, Julia is at the church, standing in front of the choir with her arms raised. I haven't been able to bring myself to attend a rehearsal; I don't want to answer everyone's questions. But booking the ticket gives me a renewed sense of determination.

I hear the choir before I get inside, their voices drifting out through the open door as I walk up the cobblestone path. I slip into a back pew in the dim church and close my eyes. They're singing "Only Time" by Enya and it makes me think of the high school choir, how George used to hide his homework behind his sheet music and scribble away at math problems. We sang "Only Time" for a year-end concert once. Enya's performance of it is haunting, but hearing it performed by multiple voices adds another layer of depth to the song.

During their break, the choir members drink water and chat. Julia notices me. She walks down the aisle and slides into the pew, placing her hand on my thigh.

It's good to see you here, she says. Rehearsal is almost over. Let's go to Kew this afternoon.

She squeezes my leg and then makes her way back down the aisle to the front of the church. Everyone picks up their songbooks again and Julia raises her arms.

After rehearsal, we walk home and grab a few things for the trip. We plan on taking a late train back, so we won't have to stay the night. I choose a book and put a few snacks in my satchel while Julia fills our water bottles. We walk to the station holding hands and Julia buys our coffee and muffins at The Runaway.

The train is quiet for a weekday afternoon. Halfway through her cup of coffee, Julia falls asleep with her head on my shoulder. The coffee cup releases gentle swirls of steam into the air from its place on the tray table. I watch the steam for a few minutes, mesmerized by its balletic arcs. Outside the window, fields and trees flash past. I plug my headphones into my phone and open YouTube. The first suggested video is the Julie Andrews concert from 1993, the one George, Kate, and I watched in the computer lab at school. I haven't watched it in years, but I click on it now and Julie Andrews appears on the screen in her gold leaf dress. My heart lifts as she stretches out her arms and twirls.

I watch the entire concert and it finishes just as we arrive at Richmond Station. Julia wakes up and stretches her arms over her head. We disembark and enter the garden through the Lion Gate. The first time I visited Kew Gardens, when I looked at the map of the sprawling three hundred acres, I wanted to hurry, to practically start running. There was too much to see and not enough time. But now I like it that parts of the place are still new to me.

We pass the Great Pagoda and walk along the Pagoda Vista towards the Temperate House. It's mid-afternoon, and there are lots of people. As Julia and I walk along the tree-lined path, I think about what life might have been like for me and Norah if we'd grown up in London instead of Prince Edward Island. I can picture us in matching school uniforms going to the art galleries with our class or riding the bus to Kew to spend the day exploring. It would have been a very different childhood, but would it have been any better?

The Temperate House is a large, ornate Victorian greenhouse. A disgruntled photographer is attempting to arrange a wedding party on the steps leading up to it. The bridesmaids, dressed in different colours, resemble a bunch of flowers. The bride takes a swig from a flask, which she extracts from within the folds of her elaborate dress. Julia tugs my arm and we continue along the path to the Palm House, which is smaller and less crowded. The geometric gardens in front of the Palm House are getting ready to bloom in shades of red and pink, and in the middle of the pond a fountain shoots water into the air.

I lead the way through the main doors, and we step into another climate. The air is filled with birdsong and with moisture that drips from the leaves of the towering palm trees. I'm transported, also, to another time. I like to picture Virginia Woolf and Vita Sackville-West boarding the bus to Kew and spending the day wandering through the Palm House, talking about writing and life and love.

The Palm House was built in 1848 and is shaped like the hull of a ship. When light filters through the thick glass, it creates an otherworldly glow. Julia and I climb the spiral staircase to the upper walkway, ascending into the tops of the trees. Even though we can hear the robins and wrens singing, they move so quickly among the trees that it's difficult to catch a glimpse. As we climb, I notice one of the staff members sitting on a bench below us, eating slices of papaya. She's holding a novel in her other hand and looks content and at home in the humid environment. She doesn't look much older than Julia, and I wonder if she always wanted to work at Kew. Maybe she visited as a young girl and was entranced by the towering palms and misty atmosphere of the Palm House, and decided right then that she would work here someday.

When we get to the top, Julia stops to take a couple of photos, while I start making my way along the walkway. There are small puddles from the mist dripping off the leaves. Gently, I touch a leaf of one of the palms and a droplet of water drips onto my hand. I could happily live in the Palm House. I could transform into a robin or a wren, build my nest among the leaves of a palm, and spend the rest of my days singing for the guests. As I stand looking down over all the foliage, without thinking too much about the consequences, I start humming a few warm-up scales and begin to sing softly. The sound, quiet as it is, bounces off the glass and floats among the trees. A few of the songbirds join in as Julia appears by my side and takes my hand. At first, I think the moisture on my cheeks is mist from the air but then I realize I'm crying.

I don't sing for very long, not wanting to push it, and when I stop the birds continue. Julia and I stay on the walkway for a long time, listening. How can I leave all this? I'm starting to feel like myself again, or at least this current version of myself, and Julia is not someone I'm willing to lose.

CHAPTER 24

Prince Edward Island, 2008 to 2009

By the time the girls started Grade Eleven, life had picked up speed. Their classmates began to talk about university and the future. Everyone had to meet with the guidance counsellor to write out a five-year plan and look at potential universities or trade programs. Ingrid saw Norah in the hallway after her appointment, and she could tell it hadn't gone well. Later, Norah was silent for their entire bus ride, but as they walked past the gas station she finally spoke.

Mrs. Jones says I need to have bigger dreams, Norah said. She stopped to watch the seagulls flapping by the dumpster. They hadn't fed them in a long time.

Why? What did you tell her? Ingrid said.

I told her that in five years I see myself still working at the bookshop, and teaching piano lessons to kids.

That's good, Ingrid said, trying to hide her excitement at

Norah's mention of the piano. Maybe there was hope they would perform together again.

I thought it was good too, but Mrs. Jones said I should think about university and should "pursue my dreams." I told her those *were* my dreams and she said I should dream bigger.

Ingrid didn't say anything. They kept walking and Ingrid linked her arm through Norah's. Norah was happy at the bookshop. Ingrid realized now that her sister had no desire to be a famous pianist, even though everyone believed she had the talent for it. But she could be many other things.

Promise me something, Norah said as they arrived at the Blue Moth and Puss greeted them in the courtyard, wrapping himself around Norah's legs.

Sure, Ingrid said. What is it?

Always come back, Norah said.

In the spring, Kate started going with Ingrid to busk downtown after school. Together, they made more money and made sure they went right to the bank machine to deposit it. If they continued at this rate, Ingrid would have enough money to go travelling. At morning choir practice, everyone asked them what it was like to sing downtown, and they made it sound more exciting than it actually was.

On Fridays, they had after-school choir practice, so they couldn't go busking. After practice, Ingrid and Kate often stayed late to talk with Mrs. Ricci. She gave them tips and lent them books to read. Her family was originally from Italy and she often went there in the summers to visit, so she told stories about the farm where they lived. Among the choir members, Mrs. Ricci was known for the click-clack of her high-heeled shoes; everyone could hear her coming before they could see her. She was a bit intimidating, but also kind, and Ingrid saw that it was possible to be both these things at once. The sound of her heels on the linoleum before practice sent everyone scrambling for their music, shoving sock feet back into shoes, chewing granola bars quickly and hiding the wrappers, covering up their overdue homework on the music stands. The choir was in full rehearsal mode for the end-of-year concert, so practices were often intense. Mrs. Ricci had high expectations, and everyone knew it.

Kate's mom let her take the truck on Fridays so she could drive home after rehearsal. But most times, Kate and Ingrid went exploring. They drove to the beach and walked the shore or went to the mall and tried on clothes they couldn't afford. These nights, Ingrid often stayed over at Kate's house. They cut holes in Kate's T-shirts to make them more edgy. The rumoured butterfly tattoo on her arm was indeed real, and when Ingrid asked if it had hurt, Kate shrugged and said not really.

At the end-of-year concert, everyone wore their nicest black clothes. Ingrid peeked around the thick red curtain and saw Norah, Elena, and Laurel in the audience, sitting a few rows back from the stage. Laurel and Norah had their heads bent together, studying the program. Elena noticed Ingrid and waved. Ingrid let the curtain fall back into place, releasing a puff of dust.

A short time later, the curtain rose and the choir filed into place. The moment before the music began was heavy and full of potential. They sang part of Mozart's *Requiem* and then a few lighter, well-known pieces. It was important, Mrs. Ricci said, to balance familiar songs with ones that had been chosen to show off their vocal talent. The second-to-last song, "A Change in Me," in which Ingrid would sing a solo, had been chosen by Mrs. Ricci. Ingrid had been secretly practising it since she started with the choir, and sometimes sang it downtown when there weren't many people around. It began with everyone singing together, but then Ingrid stepped forward under one of the hanging mics. The silence that fell in the auditorium as Ingrid began to sing alone was unlike anything she had experienced before. Everyone was holding their breath for her, and as her voice soared out into the audience, she knew for certain there was no going back.

She received a standing ovation and took a bow before stepping back in line with the rest of the choir. Kate grabbed Ingrid's hand and squeezed. The lights made it impossible to see the audience, but Ingrid heard three people cheering louder than the rest and she knew who they were.

After the final song, "There's Music in You" from Rodgers & Hammerstein's *Cinderella*, the choir dispersed backstage, talking loudly and high-fiving one another. Mrs. Ricci swooped towards Ingrid.

That's the best you've ever sung, she said.

Ingrid didn't realize she was crying until Mrs. Ricci took a tissue out of her pocket and placed it in Ingrid's hand. Kate ran up behind her and enveloped her in a hug, her chin pressing into Ingrid's shoulder.

You're a star! Kate said.

Norah appeared then, holding a bouquet of pink roses, with Laurel and Elena following behind. Norah placed the roses in Ingrid's arms. Laurel and Elena pulled the girls close and the plastic around the roses crinkled.

Let's go for ice cream, Elena said. Kate, you too.

The five of them squished into the Nissan, Ingrid sitting in the middle. She removed one rose from her bouquet and tucked it behind Norah's ear. Against her blond hair, the colour was vibrant.

At the ice cream shop, they sat in a booth instead of at the stools along the counter. The shop seemed smaller than it used to, and Ingrid realized it was because she was older now. Kate chose a song on the jukebox. The roses sat in the middle of the table and every few minutes Ingrid reached out to touch a petal.

Ada would have been so proud, Norah said, and everyone fell silent. Her name still had that power over them, an instant reminder of life before. Elena broke the silence by crunching sprinkles between her teeth. And just as she used to, when the girls were little, she grinned.

Kate found out about a party and decided they had to go. She said they had to finish the year off the right way. Ingrid wasn't sure what that meant, but she went along with it. Norah, surprisingly, agreed to go as well.

The girls got ready at Kate's house. Her mom returned from her shift at the hospital gift shop and let them go through her closet, too, to pick out something to wear. Kate's mom wasn't much older than Laurel, but she looked tired, which made her seem older. When she removed her shoes by the door, she sighed, and as she stood up straight again she held the small of her back.

Go out and have fun! she told the girls, waving them out the door.

The party was in the basement of one of the big churches downtown. A girl named Joan had stolen the key to the basement from her dad, who was the minister. One of the soccer players had an older brother who worked at a bar and had somehow procured a keg, which the boys were trying to figure out how to open when Ingrid, Norah, and Kate arrived. It was just past nine and the party had barely started. Someone plugged an iPod into some speakers and started playing rap so loud the windows rattled. The boys by the keg were shouting to be heard.

There were no more tests to study for, no more assignments to pass in. The atmosphere was light and free. The church basement smelled like old carpet, dusty books, and candles. There was macaroni art from Sunday school taped up on the walls and an upright piano in the corner. Ingrid's feet were cold in her flip-flops. The three girls chatted in a corner as more kids arrived. The boys finally got the keg open and the heavy, yeasty smell of beer filled the room as plastic cups were filled with the frothy liquid and people started dancing. A boy came over balancing three cups, which he handed to the girls.

Drink up! he said, and Kate took a big gulp. A caterpillar of white froth sat on her upper lip for a moment before she wiped it away. The boy's name was David and he was wearing a T-shirt with the Toronto Maple Leafs logo that smelled faintly of sweat. His hair was long and wavy. He kept shaking it back out of his face with a toss of his head, like a horse.

Do you like him? Ingrid asked Kate as David walked away to hand out more cups of beer. Kate shook her head and took another big swallow, looking away.

The other girls knew how to do things Ingrid didn't understand. Boys asked them to the movie theatre and the coffee shop, where they sat by the window and drank lattes like the grownups they so desperately wanted to be. Now, Ingrid watched the same girls dancing, moving their hips to the beat of the music and touching their hair. Some of the boys put their hands on the girls' waists and swayed together with them. In a dark corner, two people were kissing and Ingrid wondered what it felt like.

Kate started to dance, so Ingrid and Norah began to move too. They were awkward at first, swaying in a tight little circle without moving their arms. But as they drank more beer, their limbs became loose. There were groups of girls without boyfriends who kept glancing around the room as if looking for something. Away from school, everyone seemed more unsure of themselves. Lips painted unnatural shades of red and sparkly pink, hair piled high or hair let down, dresses and skirts shorter than usual. Everyone was a new version of themselves. Ingrid hadn't realized it was so easy to be someone different. She drank two cups of beer quickly even though she didn't like the taste. Like unbaked bread, with a bit of a sharp aftertaste. Ingrid began to feel like she was floating.

Kate noticed that Norah's dancing was getting slower, so she refilled Norah's cup.

Drink quickly! Kate said. Then you'll get drunk instead of sleepy!

Someone turned on a rotating light that threw multicoloured circles all over the walls. The circles spun and the girls danced until they were dizzy.

A slow song came on over the speakers and a few people audibly groaned but almost everyone partnered up. David appeared again and took Kate's elbow. He leaned in close and shouted something into her ear. Kate nodded and David led her to a clear space on the crowded floor. Ingrid and Norah stepped back against the wall and watched them dance, David's hands slowly moving lower and lower on Kate's back. The beer in Ingrid's cup was warm, but she drank it anyway. As Kate and David moved back and forth, with circles of light dancing across them, Ingrid realized that Kate was staring directly at her.

As the night went on, some people left and there was more room to move around. When the keg was empty, more people disappeared. Ingrid lost count of how many cups she had drunk and her feet no longer felt connected to the floor. Kate danced with David a few more times, but when he released her and disappeared into the bathroom, she came over to Ingrid and Norah. They were sitting on plastic chairs at the side of the room.

Kate reached for their hands and pulled them both to their feet, steadying Norah as she stumbled.

Come on, Kate said. I don't want to dance anymore.

Ingrid and Norah followed Kate up a back staircase to the main part of the church. It was empty, but they could hear kids outside, shouting and running around in the cemetery. Light from the street lamps shone in through the stained glass window above the altar. Kate led the way down the aisle to the front of the church and the three of them sat on the steps at the base of the podium. Ingrid leaned back on her elbows and looked up at the domed ceiling, which started to spin. Norah yelled hello and the sound echoed back. Inspired, Ingrid began to sing an Enya song they had learned in choir, and Kate and Norah joined in. Their voices rose together in harmony up into the ceiling. When the song was over Norah lay down on her side on the red velvet runner, rubbing her hand over the well-worn fabric.

Ada told us never to drink if we wanted to be professional singers, Norah said. But I like beer! Do you think this place is haunted?

Yes, definitely, Ingrid said.

Let's sleep here, Kate suggested. See if we hear any ghosts.

Norah was hesitant, but Ingrid and Kate were so eager she finally agreed. The girls huddled together on the steps, suddenly cold without the body heat from their classmates dancing around them. Ingrid's eyes were heavy with beer, her limbs made of concrete instead of air. Being drunk was okay when you were in motion, but now that she was still it was like crashing into a stone wall. She clutched Norah's damp, cold hand. After a few moments of silence, Norah's body jerked forward like she was on strings and someone had pulled them. She got to her feet, stumbled for a few steps, then vomited all over the polished wood floor.

Kate and Ingrid each took one of Norah's arms and led her to the bathroom. She drank water from the tap while Ingrid held her hair back. The bathroom was dark—the only light was from a street lamp outside—and in the mirror over the sink the three of them looked like ghosts or witches, the dark hollows of their eyes and mouths turning their faces into masks. When Norah stepped back from the sink, Ingrid took her place and started drinking. The water tasted sharp and metallic, but it made her feel better. Her stomach was bloated from the beer, and she rested her hand there. The water made a gurgling noise on its way down.

Kate splashed some water on her face. Let's go sleep, she said. I know a place.

She led Ingrid and Norah down the hallway to a small room that looked like a rehearsal space. There was a tattered, sagging sofa and a big pile of pillows. Norah curled up on the sofa in a fetal position and Ingrid sat on the other end and leaned her head back. Rummaging around in a closet, Kate found some blankets. She covered Norah with one and Norah fell asleep instantly, curled up tight like a cat.

Here, Kate said, handing Ingrid a folded blanket, which smelled musty. Ingrid took off her shoes and tucked her legs up.

Put one foot on the floor to keep the room from spinning, Kate said.

Ingrid did, and it helped. She could still hear music from below, the beat of it coming up through the sole of her bare foot like waves. Her heart was racing, as if it wanted to escape from her chest, so she wrapped her arms around her ribs and closed her eyes.

Everything looked different in the morning. Ingrid's head felt full of wet socks as she stood up from the sofa. Norah and Kate were still asleep, Norah still curled on her side, and Kate sprawled out on a makeshift bed of cushions on the floor. Ingrid tiptoed down the hallway and out a side door into the sun. Two boys lay asleep in the grass under a tree, one of them barefoot and the other shirtless. Ingrid steadied herself with one hand against a headstone and listened to the city waking up. Large leafy trees hid the cemetery from the street and softened the noise of passing cars. The world was sharp and loud and full of colour.

On the summer solstice, Ingrid, Norah, Laurel, and Elena ate breakfast together at the Blue Moth. It was getting easier to talk about Ada, but the place was still charged with her absence. The fact that she had been there one day and gone the next made it feel like she could walk back through the door at any moment. Having no gravesite to visit also made things difficult, but the girls had realized cemeteries were for the living and they were glad Ada wasn't in one.

Puss was asleep on the piano bench, curled up tight. Norah went over to pat him and he made a quiet chirping noise but kept his eyes closed. She sat on the bench next to him and slowly lifted the fallboard to reveal the piano keys. She rested her fingers on the keys. Quietly, she began to play. Scales first, then a slowed-down version of "Für Elise." From their table in the centre of the room, Ingrid, Laurel, and Elena stopped eating and listened. No one said a word. Norah played her Blue Moth piece, then played it again but quicker. Puss slept through the whole thing, unbothered. The music had been tentative and quiet at first, but the longer Norah played the more confident she seemed. When the piece finished, she left her fingers on the keys.

I'm going to give piano lessons, Norah said. She didn't turn around on the bench but made the announcement to the piano keys.

That's a great idea, Laurel said.

And that was that. Norah always did what she said she was going to do. She put up posters downtown, and within a week she had her first three students. They each came on a different day and had an hour-long session in the breakfast room. Sometimes Ingrid sat by the pool and listened as the children learned their scales and simple songs. Norah was busier than ever, between the piano lessons and the bookshop, but she looked happier than she had in a long time.

As the end of summer neared, Norah decided it was finally time to paint the floral designs on the headboards—the very last step in their long-ago project. She showed Ingrid the designs she had drawn and let Ingrid pick the colours. They went to the dollar store and bought some inexpensive acrylic paints. For just the headboards, they didn't need much of each colour. Norah traced out the designs in pencil on the wood and they draped old sheets over the beds. They each sat on their own bed and listened to the radio as they painted. Ingrid sang along to the songs she knew, and sometimes Norah joined in.

Some of the designs Norah had painted on the walls and lampshades were fading from years of being exposed to the sun, but the room was still vibrant with colour. They worked on their headboards for a few days, and when they were finished, they invited Laurel and Elena to see the final product. The four of them sat on the beds and admired the designs. Outside, it was pouring, and the surface of the pool was pockmarked and turbulent like the sea. On days like this, the Blue Moth looked more abandoned than when the sun was shining. The plastic palm trees were sun-bleached and the siding needed to be replaced. In the courtyard, weeds kept growing taller through the cracks in the pavement. Ingrid tried not to think about Fairyland and how easy it would be for the Blue Moth to fall into a similar state. Overtaken by dust and mice, as if people had never lived there at all.

CHAPTER 25

Lewes

For the first couple of seconds after I wake up in the morning, I still forget. I sit up in bed and look out at the rooftops of Lewes, the tendrils of smoke still rising from a few chimneys even though it's June. The plane ticket sits in my inbox as a reminder of my departure every time I check my email. I haven't told Julia I'm leaving, but I suspect she knows.

I reach for my laptop and begin an email to Norah but abandon it halfway through and pick up a pen and paper instead. The letter I write will arrive at the Blue Moth after I do, but I know Norah will appreciate the effort. Susan is still asleep, so in the kitchen I turn the radio on low. In the living room, the curtains are drawn, but through the fabric I can see the outlines of people walking past on their way to work. I wonder if they can see me too. This is not how any of this was supposed to go, but here I am.

I ran away from a wonderful home to see more of the world, but I've only seen one small place. I tried to become a new version of myself, but no matter where I am, I'm still just me. For a little while, when I first arrived in Lewes, I stood at the train station and sang. People tossed pound coins into my hat. In between trains, if there weren't many people waiting, I'd buy a coffee and smoke a cigarette by the corner of the building even though I knew it was bad for my voice. I've stopped that now, but when I smoked I could hear Ada telling me not to, and I liked hearing her. It scared me, how her voice was slipping away from me. Do you ever fully stop grieving for a person? Or does the grief only transform?

When Julia and I first started seeing each other, we planned a trip to Greece. We wanted to stay in a little stucco hotel in Santorini and wake up every morning to a view of the caldera glittering in the sun. I pictured a hammock on the balcony, red wine, the smell of olives, fish, and the sea. But we never got there. I never had enough money and Julia was too busy with the choir and her pottery. Instead, we spent a weekend in a little cottage by the sea in Cornwall. It rained the entire time and we stayed inside and read by the fire. With the windows open, we could smell the sea, but we only saw glimpses of it through the fog and rain.

We also went to a Florence + the Machine concert in London shortly after that. I was envious of Florence's voice, its rawness and depth of emotion. Julia and I held hands and wore glitter eyeshadow and stayed the night in a cheap hotel. The next morning, we wandered in and out of bookshops in Cecil Court wearing the same clothes as the day before.

Turning away from Susan's window, I try to decide what to do with my day. Julia is already at work in the pottery studio. The hours stretch out in front of me, empty and echoing. I decide to go for a walk across the Downs.

It's sunny and warm, so there are lots of people out with walking sticks, wearing practical hiking boots. I ruffle the fur of a few dogs who brush against my legs.

I walk in the direction of Rodmell and end up on the road which leads to Monk's House, the country home of Virginia Woolf. The pub at the top of the road is getting ready to open for lunch—staff are moving back and forth behind the windows. Monk's House is run by the National Trust and is open to tours, but today it's closed and the narrow streets of Rodmell are quiet. A few people wearing High-Vis vests ride past on their horses, the clip-clop of hooves against pavement the only sound on this otherwise sleepy stretch. I try to remember what day of the week it is but can't be sure if it's Monday or Tuesday.

The Monk's House garden and Woolf's writing studio back onto the churchyard and I sit on the low stone wall under the giant chestnut tree. As I settle in, I see a flash of colour moving along the lane. A woman in a bright scarf is walking away from me. A scarf like Ada would have worn, the wind lifting it into the air. There was no one in the yard when I walked through, so she must have come from inside the church. For a moment, I consider following her, but she disappears from sight.

Sunlight filters through the leaves of the chestnut tree. In the nearby field, cows moo and shuffle in the grass. I like to think not much has changed since Woolf lived here, but I know that's not true. Things change so slowly we don't even notice. But some things remain, like this chestnut tree and that little shed where so many books were written. I startle when a brown cat jumps up on the wall next to me. The cat rubs against my arm and I stroke her head. She sits down beside me and looks into the garden as if waiting for someone.

CHAPTER 26

Prince Edward Island, 2009 to 2010

One morning at the beginning of Grade Twelve, Mrs. Ricci made an announcement during choir practice. The choir would be applying for a place in an international competition to be held in May in London, England. Everyone started talking at once, and she clapped her hands sharply. She looked stern, but Ingrid could sense that she was just as excited as they were. She said they'd have to practise harder than ever before to make it into the competition.

I believe in you, Mrs. Ricci told them as she gazed around the room. All of you.

When they weren't in the rehearsal room, Ingrid, Kate, and George watched more videos on the school computers. They looked up all the other choirs that would most likely apply to the competition and studied their performances.

One day at lunch, George and Kate were on fundraising duty

in the cafeteria so Ingrid was alone in the rehearsal room. She was eating a sandwich, her book propped open on her music stand, when Mrs. Ricci entered the room. Ingrid had been so absorbed in her novel she hadn't even heard the famous shoes.

Oh, hello Ingrid! I didn't know anyone was in here.

Sorry, I'll leave. Ingrid fumbled to put her sandwich back in its wrapper.

No, stay, Mrs. Ricci said as she sat down at her desk.

It grew awkward in the room, with only the sound of Ingrid's chewing and swallowing. So she started to talk. She told Mrs. Ricci about the Julie Andrews concert she had watched online, and the Around the World game, and how going to London would be a dream come true. She told her about Ada teaching her to sing and teaching Norah how to play the piano, and it seemed right to say Ada's name aloud.

Ada and I were friends a long time ago, Mrs. Ricci said. She was the one who recommended me for this job. I'm very sorry for your loss.

Ingrid didn't know what to say. She looked down.

We sang together in high school, Mrs. Ricci explained. Then Ada went away to university in London, to study voice, and we fell out of touch. When she moved back and had your mother, we started visiting each other on the weekends, walking around the city. But then—Mrs. Ricci stops, like it's her turn to not know what to say. Then Ada lost her parents and inherited the Blue Moth. And Laurel was still very young. Then she lost her husband.

Mrs. Ricci looked directly at Ingrid. But I'm sure you know all this, she said.

Ingrid shook her head. No. Nobody really talks about stuff.

That must be hard, Mrs. Ricci said. Ada was a very private person, and she went through a lot in her life. But she loved

Laurel, and she loved you and your sister.

Ingrid had never known that Ada went to school in London, had lived a whole other life before the Blue Moth Motel. There were so many things Ingrid wanted to ask Ada, but it was too late. She could ask Mrs. Ricci, though.

Why didn't Ada go back to London? Ingrid asked.

I think her connection to here was too strong, Mrs. Ricci said. She loved the island; it was her home. Sometimes, we have to decide what and who to love. And the decision is never easy.

Ingrid pictured Ada at seventeen or eighteen in a long black dress, singing with a choir in a church in London. A big church. A cathedral. What did it feel like to look up at the cathedral ceiling and hear her voice echo back? Ingrid wanted to hear Ada's voice soar. It made her sad to know she could never meet that version of her grandmother, the one who had her whole life ahead of her. But Ingrid could do one thing for Ada: she could sing.

She would go to London, too, and study voice.

Before school let out for Christmas, the choir recorded their audition tape for the competition so Mrs. Ricci could send it away. Ingrid stayed afterwards and Mrs. Ricci helped her make an audition tape to send to universities.

I'll write you a letter of recommendation as well, Mrs. Ricci said as she handed Ingrid the memory stick which contained the possibility of her future.

At the Blue Moth, Ingrid helped Norah, Laurel, and Elena decorate for Christmas. Even though they'd be having their dinner at Ada's bungalow, it seemed wrong not to string the garlands and put the tree up in the breakfast room. Ingrid sang the audition songs over and over until Norah begged her to stop.

When the four of them sat down for Christmas dinner, Ingrid told them she wanted to apply to universities in the UK.

You haven't even visited yet, Laurel said as she sliced her carrots. Maybe wait and see if the choir gets to go before you make your decision.

Elena reached over and put her hand on top of Ingrid's. You still have lots of time.

But Ingrid didn't feel like she had lots of time. She felt like the only one who realized how fast life moved, how easy it was to disappear. Ada had disappeared, and Ingrid believed if she kept moving, kept singing, a little piece of Ada would stay with them forever.

I think it's a great idea, Laurel said as she laid her cutlery down and got up from the table. I know I've always wanted to see London.

She took her plate back into the kitchen and Ingrid heard the dishwasher door open and shut, then the glug of more wine being poured into a glass. When Laurel stepped back into the dining room, she was trying to smile.

Ingrid was grateful to return to school in January. When classes ended the first day, Norah went to the bookshop while Ingrid went to choir practice. Everyone spoke in hushed, excited voices as they waited for Mrs. Ricci. George heard her approaching first and signalled for everyone to shush. When she walked through the door, the room was silent and she paused at the threshold.

We're going to London! she said, waving a piece of paper in the air.

Fundraising efforts amped up and the choir set up a table in the cafeteria for donations. Every Friday they had a bake sale. The school would pay for accommodations and food, but everyone had to pay their own airfare. People took turns at the fundraising table, and within a few months they had raised enough money to help with everyone's costs. The kids who were on duty at the table would play music from their phones on a small Bluetooth speaker. Sometimes Ingrid sang along. She didn't care what anyone thought anymore. She was going to sing in London. Without telling anyone other than Mrs. Ricci, Ingrid had applied to the University of Sussex and the Royal Academy of Music. The international student fees were terrifying; they made Ingrid feel jittery. It was expensive even to apply.

≡

Ingrid and Kate decided to sing downtown again in the early spring. They hadn't busked there since the fall because Mrs. Ricci had warned them against singing when it was too cold. But Ingrid needed to save more money. As they walked along the waterfront, Ingrid noticed a woman outside a large white house that overlooked the harbour. She was kneeling in a flower bed under a window, green plastic knee pads on over faded blue jeans. Ingrid stopped and grabbed Kate's arm.

Isn't that Mrs. Ricci?

The two-storey house had large, white columns flanking the front door, which was painted red. All the shrubs on the front lawn were still wrapped in burlap, even though the risk of it snowing again was low. Old, thick trees had been planted strategically on the lawn, surrounded by circular beds which would be full of flowers come summer. A restored antique truck was parked in front of the garage.

Does she live here? Kate said.

The two of them stood awkwardly on the sidewalk, partially hidden by a large bush on the neighbour's lawn, and watched

Mrs. Ricci planting bulbs. Seeing her in gardening clothes instead of a schoolteacher outfit made her seem like a character in a different story.

Let's go say hi, Ingrid said.

They continued along the sidewalk and started up the walkway to Mrs. Ricci's house. She heard them and turned, smiling. In one fluid motion, she stood and brushed the soil off her jeans.

Hello, you two! she said. What brings you down this way?

We're going to sing, Kate said. But then we saw you, so we decided to stop and say hi.

Well, perfect timing, Mrs. Ricci said. I was just going to take a break. Come on in.

They followed her through a side door and hovered as she removed her knee pads and set them on a wooden table. She took her shoes off and put them under the table, so the girls did the same. It was even more strange to see Mrs. Ricci in sock feet. Nearby, a pair of sheepskin slippers sat waiting, and she slid them on. Ingrid stared down at her own socks and was glad there were no holes in them. As they followed Mrs. Ricci into the kitchen, Ingrid tried to look around without being obvious.

This was my parents' house, Mrs. Ricci said. I've kept it mostly to their taste, which is thankfully very similar to mine.

The kitchen was large, with a big wooden table and a black-and-white checkered floor. Papers and books covered half the table and there was a green cardigan draped over the back of one of the chairs. The counters were spotless. Mrs. Ricci washed her hands in the sink and dried them on a gingham towel hanging on the handle of the oven. The walls were painted soft yellow and the room smelled faintly of Pine-Sol.

Mrs. Ricci filled a kettle with water, while Ingrid and Kate sat down at the table. They glanced at the piles of sheet music, academic articles, and university booklets. Mrs. Ricci took three mugs out of the cupboard and a jug of milk from the fridge.

My husband works late these days, Mrs. Ricci said. I don't make supper until much later. I like a bit of tea to tide me over.

Ingrid tried to take in as many details about the kitchen as she could, so she could tell Norah later. She wanted to know about the multicoloured ceramic sugar bowl and what Mrs. Ricci was going to make for supper. Her teacher's life seemed flawless, and Ingrid wanted to know how she had created it, and if it was possible to be someone like Ingrid and end up being someone like Mrs. Ricci. The more she listened to Mrs. Ricci speak, the more Ingrid wondered about Ada's life before the Blue Moth. It was easy to picture Ada in a house like this, walking down the staircase in the morning with a scarf tied around her hair, to tend the flowers in the garden. Was life at the Blue Moth what Ada had wanted? Or had she wanted something else, but hadn't had the choice?

Do you think Ada would have gone back to London if she hadn't inherited the Blue Moth? Ingrid asked Mrs. Ricci.

I like to think so, Mrs. Ricci said. We were going to go back together. But plans don't always work out.

Ingrid and Kate talked with Mrs. Ricci for about an hour. She tried to answer all their questions about London, which she often visited en route to Italy. Then she turned to Kate and asked what she wanted to do after graduation. Kate said she wanted to be a marine biologist and study horseshoe crabs or giant squid. Everyone else wanted to study whales or colourful tropical fish, but Kate wasn't interested in those.

Horseshoe crabs have a horseshoe-shaped body, hence the name, Kate said. And they have blue blood. She pulled up a picture on her phone.

But I'm also fascinated by the giant squid, Kate added. Ingrid thought of how Kate only used words like *fascinated* when she was around teachers. Mrs. Ricci made everyone want to be more sophisticated.

Scientists don't know much about them, Kate was saying. I saw one in formaldehyde once, at a museum in St. John's. I want to be the one who discovers more clues about their lives.

The giant squid has long tentacles, eyes the size of basketballs, and three hearts, Kate explained. As Ingrid listened, she wondered what humans would be like if they had three hearts instead of only one.

≡≡≡

Ingrid marked off every day on the calendar with a red X, and before she knew it, the date of their departure for London arrived. She had packed and unpacked her bag half a dozen times to make sure she didn't forget anything, spent hours on the phone with Kate planning their outfits and what books they would bring. It would be Ingrid's first time on a plane, her first time away from home without Norah. But she was excited more than nervous, because she was doing what she and Norah had always planned.

When Norah realized how many times Ingrid had packed and unpacked, she offered to do it for her. She folded Ingrid's clothes neatly and tucked them into the small suitcase.

Ingrid wanted to say so many things. She wanted to apologize for not understanding grief, never knowing how to live with it, never knowing what to say. She was sorry for trying to make Norah sing when she didn't want to sing and trying to make her play piano and perform together. For not accepting that they wanted different things from life.

Laurel, Elena, and Norah took Ingrid to the airport. It wasn't a long drive, and the Charlottetown airport is small. The four of them embraced near the security doors and Norah tried hard not to cry. Mrs. Ricci and the rest of the choir were in the security line. Kate kept looking over her shoulder, waiting for Ingrid. Finally, Ingrid pulled her little rolling suitcase behind her and waved as she stepped through the sliding doors. Through the frosted glass, she could see the outline of the three of them still standing on the other side.

It was late when they arrived in London. Everyone was bleary-eyed with tired, creased faces. Ingrid was stiff from sitting still, so she was happy to walk around while they waited for their luggage to come off the plane. Then they followed Mrs. Ricci to what seemed to be the basement of the airport and into what she called the Tube station, where they lined up to buy transit passes that were for some reason called Oyster cards. Underground, the air smelled stale and the whoosh of the arriving train made Ingrid stumble. Mrs. Ricci took her elbow, telling her to be careful. On the Tube, Ingrid stood in the luggage area with her suitcase on the floor between her feet. She held onto the bar in front of her with both hands, but when the train lurched into motion she almost lost her balance again. A few of the others also held on tightly, trying to absorb the sway of the Tube through their legs.

They were staying in a student hostel close to the British Museum. It was past midnight when they emerged from the station, and again Mrs. Ricci led the way. It was starting to remind Ingrid of that children's book about the girls in Paris who follow their teacher in two straight lines. Brick buildings and row houses lined the street and the unfamiliar shriek of a siren made Ingrid jump as they walked past a twenty-four-hour grocery store.

Ingrid and Kate were sharing a room at the hostel. When they stepped inside, Ingrid went straight to the window and threw back the curtains, expecting an expansive view of tall buildings, or maybe a Mary Poppins streetscape. Instead, she saw the brick wall of the building next door. Their room was small and narrow, with two single beds pushed up against opposite walls and just enough space for a small table between them. There was one bathroom for the entire floor. Kate flopped onto one of the beds and said she felt like she was at summer camp. Ingrid agreed, even though she had never been to summer camp. They unpacked a few things and changed into their pajamas. Kate had a small Bluetooth speaker, so she turned on some music, but she had to turn it off again when someone in the next room started banging on the wall. Even though the bathroom was at the end of the hallway, Ingrid could hear it every time someone flushed. It was nearly two a.m. when they went to bed and Ingrid knew she should be exhausted but she couldn't close her eyes. She didn't want to miss anything.

There were two days for sightseeing before the competition. Two parent chaperones had come along to help, so that meant the choir members got three choices of where to go. They all met in the hostel cafeteria in the morning for a breakfast buffet and to split into groups. There were baked beans, toast, eggs, sausages, and cereal. A bottomless supply of coffee led to many jittery, over-excited singers. Kate and Ingrid chose to join Mrs. Ricci's group to see the art galleries and Kew Gardens.

On the way to the National Gallery, they walked past a few bookshops and Ingrid snapped a picture of each one to show Norah. There were people everywhere, more than Ingrid had ever seen in one place in her entire life—she loved the rush of being one person in a large crowd. The fountain in Trafalgar Square sent a fine mist into the air and Ingrid closed her eyes as it landed on her cheeks and hair. A group of young school children dressed in navy blue uniforms crossed the square among all the tourists on their way to the gallery.

Mrs. Ricci set them free in the gallery with instructions to meet in the gift shop in three hours. Every room had the hushed atmosphere of a church. Ingrid started off trying to look at every painting, but she quickly became overwhelmed. The Impressionists worked in pale, muted colours, and everything appeared slightly out of focus. She found the paintings she had first seen as prints on Ada's wall and wrote down the names of the artists so she could look them up later.

Ingrid decided, as she walked slowly through the gallery, that she would live in London no matter what. It was the first real city she had visited and she wanted to know all its secrets. She and Norah had taken so many art books out of the library over the years, but seeing the paintings in person made Ingrid want to reach out and feel the texture of the paint.

They ate in Leicester Square on benches by the fountain. Even though it was only May, the air was warm and humid like summer. Squirrels and pigeons darted around everyone's feet. Ingrid ate an avocado and chicken sandwich, the first time she had eaten avocado. It tasted tropical and mushy, like a banana. She thought that whenever she ate avocado in her life, she would remember that first day in London.

After lunch, they walked to the Tate Modern. Ingrid focused on one painting in every room rather than trying to take in everything. In one room, her eye was caught by a painting of a woman in a white dress standing next to a cello. There was something about how the woman was staring out from the canvas directly at the viewer. Ingrid had never been watched by a painting, and she stood there for a long time, meeting the woman's gaze.

The day before the competition, Mrs. Ricci and six of the choir members boarded a red double-decker bus to Kew Gardens. Ingrid and Kate climbed the narrow spiral staircase to the second level and sat in the very front seats so they could get the best view. Branches scraped against the side of the bus, and when they went around corners Ingrid was convinced it was going to tip over. Along the way, Mrs. Ricci pointed out the sights like a tour guide: churches and art galleries and little shops she had been to over the years.

At Kew, the group had to stick together so no one would get lost. There wasn't enough time to see everything. When they walked through the doors of the Palm House, Ingrid stopped and looked up at the canopy of palm trees, the first real ones she had ever seen. The air was full of birdsong. Sun beamed down through the glass and the light was an amphibious green, like being underwater in a murky pond. A wrought iron spiral staircase led to an upper walkway, and Ingrid couldn't resist it. She climbed until she was level with the treetops, Kate following behind her on the narrow treads. Palm fronds draped over the walkway at the top, and water dripped from leaves and fell into puddles at Ingrid and Kate's feet. The other four choir members had joined them on the walkway. Quietly at first, Ingrid began to sing the first thing that came into her head—"Only Time" by Enya, which they would sing at the competition. Kate joined in almost immediately, followed by the others. They stood in a group on the walkway, hidden among the palms, and sang the entire song. Somewhere down below, Mrs. Ricci looked up. Several visitors also stopped to listen, trying to locate the source of the music. The moist air absorbed the sound and bounced their voices around so it sounded like they were singing from everywhere at the same time. When the song was over, the people below applauded and you could hear the birds chirping again.

Ingrid hadn't realized how nervous she was about the competition. But with the song out of her system, she was calm and prepared. Ingrid held onto the railing and looked out over the tops of the trees as the others moved on. The greenhouse was large, but it was only one small place in the world. There were many other places Ingrid would never visit, many views she wouldn't see. When she and Norah were young, they had thought there was so much time. Maybe learning as much as possible about one place could be just as worthwhile as learning a few things about hundreds of places. She wondered if Ada had ever been to Kew. It was easy to picture her here, among the leaves and flowers, catching glimpses of birds as they flitted through the light.

Mrs. Ricci appeared by Ingrid's side and put a hand on her arm.

Do you love it? Mrs. Ricci asked.

Yes, Ingrid said. I want to live here.

Right here? Mrs. Ricci gestured at the treetops.

Yes, right here in the trees with the birds.

A few of them sat in the courtyard behind the hostel that evening, talking and drinking strange flavours of juice from the vending machine. Ingrid looked up at the London sky as it faded to a dusky purple. She didn't want to go back to the Blue Moth. There were new versions of herself to discover in each new place.

On the pay phone in the lobby, Ingrid called Norah and was shocked by how close she sounded, as if she was in the next room instead of across the ocean.

Is it everything we hoped it would be? Norah said.

There was something sad in her voice. Ingrid wanted to reach through the phone and pull her through to the other side. Norah deserved to see everything, too. All the art and music and the sky through the leaves of the ancient ginkgo tree at Kew Gardens. Ingrid told her how the paintings have texture and look different up close, how some of them were much bigger than she expected and hung in heavy, ornate frames.

But is it as good as we dreamed it would be? Norah asked again.

Yes, Ingrid said. It's everything.

The morning of the competition dawned rainy and grey. Mrs. Ricci seemed exhilarated by this and kept saying it was a perfect London day. Everyone ate baked beans on toast and did vocal warm-up exercises in the lobby until the woman at the front desk asked them to stop. Dressed in black pants and a freshly pressed white button-down shirt, Ingrid looked more like a server than a singer. She tied her tie, which was Prince Edward Island tartan, and helped Kate tie hers. The girls had pulled their hair back into buns at the base of their necks, but Ingrid couldn't get all her curls to lie flat. She smoothed the flyaways at her temple.

They caught the bus to the cathedral where the competition would take place. Each choir had a small area in the basement where they could warm up and wait their turn. They were scheduled to perform third, which pleased Mrs. Ricci. She said going early in the day meant the examiners were still fresh. The faint sound of the first two choirs leaked down through the ceiling, but Mrs. Ricci told them not to listen.

You can listen to the other groups after you've performed, she said. It will influence your voices if you hear them now.

Ingrid thought Mrs. Ricci was worried that if they heard

how polished the other choirs were, and how many songs they performed in different languages, they would start to doubt themselves.

You are all beautiful, capable singers, Mrs. Ricci said as they prepared to take the stage. And we're not here to win, we're here for the experience. Remember that.

Ingrid's hands were shaking as they stood on the velvet-carpeted chancel and faced the pews. The cathedral was a stunning example of Gothic architecture, according to Mrs. Ricci, and Ingrid stared up at the ornate stained glass windows and the soaring domed ceiling. She pictured her voice floating up there, bouncing off the dome. Her voice could travel places she could not; all she had to do was let it go.

Mrs. Ricci took her place in front of the choir and raised her hands. There was a moment of complete silence, and then they began. On the first song they faltered a bit as their voices adjusted to the cavernous space. But by the time they reached the Enya song, their voices were clear and true. Ingrid watched Mrs. Ricci, the way her arms moved and how she mouthed the words with them. And that was when Ingrid felt it: all of their voices clicked together and they became one flawless organism. It was as if her feet had lifted off the ground and she was floating up to the ceiling with her voice.

The first two choirs, who were watching from the pews, clapped and cheered when they finished singing. Sweat dripped down Ingrid's back and her cheeks hurt but she had never felt so much a part of something as she did in that moment. As the choir filed off the stage, Ingrid reached for Kate's hand and pulled her away from the group and down a back hallway she had noticed on their way up. The door at the end opened into a courtyard with rhododendron bushes and flagstones, glossy in the rain that was coming down. There was a rickety patio set and a chipped bird bath, overflowing. The courtyard was enclosed by tall stone walls. In the doorway, Ingrid took off her shoes and stepped out into it.

You're getting soaked! Kate said.

But Ingrid didn't care. The cool rain refreshed her sweaty skin. She tipped her head back to the sky and stretched out her arms.

When the choir returned from London, Ingrid found out she hadn't been accepted by either of the universities she had applied to. The rejection letters sat on the table in the breakfast room for weeks, the envelopes ripped open and discarded. Ingrid read them every morning, as if searching for clues. The choir competition had been such a high and Ingrid thought for certain her whole life had opened up in front of her. But here she was with her rejection letters and the sympathetic faces of her family. She dreaded telling Mrs. Ricci, so she put it off.

It was a warm spring, but rather than spending time outside, Ingrid closed the curtains and stayed in. At the Blue Moth, a standing fan pushed the humid, stale air around the room and Ingrid sweated in the dim light. Once classes were over, her only excursion was a walk to the library now and then to get another pile of books. She ate sporadically, usually when Norah or Kate dragged her off the bed and out into the courtyard, where they sat in the old plastic chairs by the pool and balanced plates in their laps. Kate seemed like she never knew what to say, and there was something disjointed again between Norah and Ingrid, a certain wariness around each other. Puss would sit by Norah's chair and look up at her expectantly, waiting for a treat. Sometimes Laurel and Elena would join them and drink mojitos, chewing the mint leaves like gum.

The smell from the sewage lagoon was more frequent than usual that year. The pool wasn't filled yet, even though the weather was warm enough, and seagulls splashed in the dirty water that had collected in the plastic cover.

Ingrid and Norah had become "the girls who used to perform at the pub." Ingrid was "the girl who used to sing downtown." Just like the Blue Moth "used to" be an actual motel. In a place like this, where people tended to stay put, things were defined by their "used to be's." Like "drive past where the liquor store used to be and take your first right." The rest of her family seemed determined to live in the past, where things were familiar. But Ingrid didn't want to be defined by things she used to do.

On the last day before the teachers and staff left school, Ingrid went in to meet with the guidance counsellor to talk about her plans to take a year off. Since she hadn't applied to any backup schools, it was too late to be accepted elsewhere. Kate was going to the local university and Norah was sticking to her book-shop-and-piano-lessons plan. But Ingrid was treading water, waiting to be told which direction to swim in, in order to reach the shore. The guidance counsellor looked at Ingrid over the top of her glasses. She handed her some pamphlets for Canadian schools with music programmes, schools she could apply to next year. As she left the room, Ingrid shoved the pamphlets down to the bottom of her backpack. Then she went to the rehearsal room.

Mrs. Ricci was there, sitting at her desk. She looked up when Ingrid came in and gestured for her to take a seat.

I didn't get in, Ingrid said.

I know, Mrs. Ricci said.

Mrs. Ricci opened her desk drawer and Ingrid looked up. On the desk, Mrs. Ricci placed an old photograph of two young women standing outside a church. Their arms were linked at the elbow and a little bit blurred, as if they were moving them when the photo was taken. Ada's curly hair and round eyes were unmistakable. The other woman had darker, long hair and was a bit taller. It was the same photograph Ingrid had seen framed on Ada's wall, but this copy was in colour and it was easier to tell who the women were. Still, Ingrid took the photograph and flipped it over to read the names. *Ada and Laura, London.*

Go anyway, Mrs. Ricci said.

———

Ingrid's flight was scheduled for late August, just before her eighteenth birthday. With Mrs. Ricci's help, Ingrid had found a room to rent in Lewes, a historic town Ingrid had read about in connection to Virginia Woolf. It was just an hour away from London. Ingrid wrote the address on a slip of paper which she attached to the fridge with a magnet. That slip of paper was the only reminder of Ingrid's departure because no one wanted to talk about it, but everything Ingrid did that summer felt different. She wanted to take everything in, store every detail in her head so when she closed her eyes she could still see it.

It rained a lot that summer, so the girls spent most of their free time inside at the bungalow watching movies. Being in the house still felt as if they were living someone else's life. It didn't help that the furniture reminded them so much of Ada, even though they hadn't spent much time in the bungalow when they were growing up. Ingrid took the photograph of Ada and Mrs. Ricci off the wall and told Norah the story. She held the photograph in her lap and stared at the young women in the image for a long time before she spoke.

Do you think they loved each other? Norah said.

Yes, Ingrid answered. And as she said the word, she knew it was true.

But they both married other people.

I think it was complicated for them, Ingrid said. And I think it's possible to love more than one person.

The girls took the photograph back to the Blue Moth and Norah put it on the piano.

In July, after a month of cold swims and rainy beach walks, Ingrid was reading in their room at the Blue Moth one afternoon when Norah entered with an envelope. She handed it to her sister, and Ingrid sat up to open it. Inside was a slip of paper with a reservation for two at Arabella by the Sea, the place where they had once dreamed of living. Someone from the States had bought the inn and it had been open again for a few years.

Happy early birthday, Norah said. Since you'll be far away when it's your real birthday.

Ingrid stood up and hugged her sister tight.

A couple of weekends later, Ingrid and Norah found themselves on the top floor at Arabella by the Sea, in the same room they'd gone into all those years ago. Ingrid threw open the balcony doors and stood outside in the sunshine. There was a vase of fresh flowers on the bedside table and the room smelled like lavender and the sea.

What this place is really missing is the smell of sewage, Ingrid said from the balcony.

Down in the dining room, a fire roared in the stone hearth even though it was August. Everyone was dressed in clean blues and whites, like some sort of country club. Norah and Ingrid had their bathing suits on, under jean shorts and tank tops. The host, in his immaculate khakis and pale blue button-down, glared at Ingrid's flip-flops as if he was personally offended by the sound they made when she walked. But the hostess sat them at a round table by the window and poured their water. Outside, children played bocci on the lawn and for a moment Ingrid wanted to be out there with them.

Maybe I won't go, Ingrid said as Norah took a sip of water.

What do you mean?

It's beautiful here. Why do I want to leave? I don't know anymore.

Norah was quiet for a moment. She set her water glass down and followed Ingrid's gaze out the window.

We can't stay children forever, she said. It was fun, but I think being any age can be fun.

At least we can have cake for breakfast, Ingrid said.

And lobster, Norah said as the server appeared balancing two plates with a large red crustacean perched on each of them.

It was the first time either of the girls had eaten lobster. Even in a place where it was so abundant, the idea of a lobster supper seemed extravagant and out of reach. But as Ingrid looked around the dining room at all the other people eating, butter dripping down their chins despite their elegant outfits, it didn't seem so extravagant anymore. The cracking of claws was interspersed with conversation and some of the diners wore plastic bibs with a picture of a cartoon lobster.

Norah convinced the young server to bring a bottle of champagne to their table. He was a student working a summer job and didn't ask to see IDs. When he left to get the bottle, Ingrid kicked Norah's foot.

What? Norah said as she smoothed a napkin over her lap.

Apparently your smile is very convincing, Ingrid said.

I was just being nice.

Sure, sure, Ingrid said.

The champagne arrived in a bucket of ice with two crystal glasses. The sky outside turned pink and orange, then lilac and grey as the sun faded and disappeared. The champagne made Ingrid giddy, the bubbles fizzing in her throat. They drank half the bottle while they ate and when Norah stood up from the table an hour later, she hiccupped and turned bright red.

They took the bottle upstairs. Norah's eyes shone and she kept touching her collarbone with one hand. She collapsed on the bed and Ingrid went out onto the balcony to look at the sea.

Norah was sound asleep when Ingrid stepped back into the room. She left the balcony doors open and put a plaid wool blanket over Norah. Quietly, Ingrid changed into her pajamas and crawled into the cloud of a bed, careful not to disturb her sister. The sea was audible through the open doors.

Ingrid woke up shortly after midnight and found herself alone in the bed. Confused, she slipped into one of the complimentary robes that were waiting in the closet. She opened the door of their room and peered down the hallway, which was lit with a soft golden glow. Everything was quiet. Her head was still fuzzy and full from the champagne, and it seemed as if she was floating as she made her way downstairs. Even though supper had ended hours ago, the fire still crackled in the grate in the dining room. The baby grand gleamed in the firelight and Norah's fingers were moving tentatively on the keys. She was playing more quietly than usual, so as not to wake any of the guests. Ingrid stood with her back to the fire, far enough away that Norah didn't know she was there. The piece was unfamiliar to Ingrid, a slow, melancholy melody. As she listened, she could pick up something hesitant, or, more than that, exploratory, in her sister's playing. Ingrid realized that Norah was making it up as she went.

CHAPTER 27

Lewes

The evening before I'm due to fly home, I wander the streets and stare in at lighted windows. People are making supper, sitting down at their tables and pouring wine. I glance into each house as I pass, even though the curtains are pulled tight in some windows and all I can see is the glow of light. The mundane nature of it all comforts me, makes me feel a bit like myself again.

My voice is getting stronger. Last week at the doctor's office, I was cleared to start doing light vocal exercises again. I thought about cancelling my ticket. But Norah would never forgive me for missing the party, so I kept the ticket.

I go to my favourite bench down by the river and stare at the swirling water for a little while. At night, if the moon is full, sometimes it looks as if the chalk hills are glowing and the river is blue. But there's cloud cover tonight and the water is inky and deep. Nearby, on the other side of the river, Julia is sitting on her sofa, reading, or maybe she's pulling a late night out in the pottery shed making a new set of mugs. I could go to her, sit next to her on the sofa or watch the pottery wheel spin round and round under her hands. But I want to spend my last night here on my own. The world I've created is expanding in front of me, becoming something new. But for now, it's time to go home.

———

I meet Julia at our favourite breakfast spot by the water and we sit in our regular corner booth. I have my suitcase and backpack with me. She reaches across the table and takes hold of both my hands.

I'm going to miss you, okay? she says. You have to come back.

I will. I promise.

Satisfied, Julia leans back and looks at the menu even though we always get the same thing. The server arrives with two lattes in bowl-sized mugs and takes the order: eggs benedict for both of us.

When's your train? Julia asks, even though she knows the answer, has asked me this question a dozen times in the past few days.

Ten o'clock, I say. We still have lots of time.

Here, Julia says, I made you this.

She takes a mug out of her shoulder bag and places it on the table. It's a similar shape to her green ones, round and easy to hold. The base is terracotta and the body is pale blue, almost grey. I cradle it in my hands. It's lighter than it looks.

Thank you, it's perfect.

Wrap it up carefully in your luggage, Julia says. So it doesn't break.

CHAPTER 28

Prince Edward Island, 2013

I fly into Halifax first and change planes. The one to Charlotte-town has nine seats on either side, so everyone is by a window. We fly low, close enough to see the water of the Northumber-land Strait. I almost press my face against the window to catch the first glimpse of red clay. From above, the island is a patchwork quilt of green fields interspersed with veins of red dirt roads which end at the sparkling sea. The rising sun turns the cabin of the plane gold as we descend to the airport.

I climb down the metal steps to the tarmac and breathe deeply. Seaweed and red clay, the only place in the world that smells like this. By the end of summer, sometimes the air smells vaguely like compost from the seaweed having spent a few months in the sun. But in June it smells fresh and salty.

As soon as I enter the terminal, I see my family standing together, waiting for me. It's been nearly three years, except for a quick visit home the first Christmas. Norah's in the middle, and she's the one who sees me first. Laurel starts crying, though she's trying not to. When I reach them, Elena touches my hair, which is much shorter than it used to be. Norah's eyes are swimming.

Welcome home, she says.

When my single suitcase arrives on the luggage carousel, I catch Norah looking at Laurel with a question in her eyes, but she doesn't say anything.

Laurel and Elena's car, a blue Hyundai, is parked in the lot out front. Norah owns Ada's Cadillac now, which runs well despite its age. Elena lifts my suitcase into the trunk while Norah and I climb into the back and Laurel slides into the driver's seat. She slaps her hands on the steering wheel and we're off. Lupins line the side of the highway, bright patches of purple, pink, and white. All the colours of home—the vibrant greens, red clay, and blue ocean—look even brighter than I remember. The drive from the airport to the Blue Moth takes about twenty minutes, and the four of us spend the entire time singing along to the radio rather than talking. Laurel rolls all the windows down so the car becomes a wind tunnel. I sing quietly, my voice still uncertain. The reedy sound scares me a bit, but I like hearing Norah's voice rise over mine.

When we stop for gas, seagulls are squawking by the dumpsters. With the windows down, the familiar smells of the sewage lagoon and gasoline fill my nose like liquid. Norah is worried we won't have enough marshmallows and pop for the party, so she goes into the gas station to buy more. I remain in the car with Elena while Laurel pumps the gas. Elena turns the radio down and turns in her seat to face me.

I'm glad you're home, she says.

Me too.

Norah returns with her provisions and Laurel goes inside to

pay. When everyone is back in the car, there's a strange silence.

What? I say. What is it?

I guess you'll see soon enough, Laurel says as she starts the car.

We drive the short distance from the gas station to the Blue Moth, and as we pull into the driveway I see the sign. The bold red words "For Sale" stand out against the faded blue siding and I look at Norah.

Why is there a for sale sign? I say, hating the question as soon as it comes out of my mouth.

It's Laurel who answers. It's time, she says. She pulls into the parking spot outside the breakfast room and Puss comes trotting around the corner to meet us. I hear the familiar gurgle of the pool but I notice the plastic palm trees are missing. Norah gets out of the car and scoops Puss up in her arms, burying her face in his fur. He lives with Norah in her apartment above the bookshop, but I guess she's brought him here for now, so that truly everyone will be together.

The engine ticks as Elena gets out and opens the trunk to get my suitcase. I remain in the car with Laurel, who stares out the windshield at Norah as she carries Puss into the breakfast room.

We need to move on, Laurel says finally. The smell gets worse every year now. Sometimes even I can barely stand it. But we opened the pool for you.

Where are the palm trees? I ask.

We had to take them down. The plastic was all cracked and faded, Laurel says. We've had a few low offers, one from the man who owns the gas station, but I know all he wants to do is tear it down to expand his parking lot.

I picture a wrecking ball smashing into the side of the Blue Moth, the walls crumpling in on themselves. I get out of the car, grab my backpack, and go into the breakfast room to find Norah.

She's sitting on the piano bench with her fingers hovering over the keys. Puss is lying under the bench, already asleep. I sit down next to my sister. Her shoulders are tight, almost touching her ears, and there are tracks of tears down her cheeks. She takes a deep breath to relax and starts to play the piece she wrote for Ada. As I listen, I pretend we've gone back in time.

A couple of hours later, I wake up from a nap in our old room. I'd fallen asleep on top of the duvet with my shoes on. My suitcase and backpack are by the door, still packed. Everything is the same but there's a layer of dust on all the furniture and it feels too quiet. Our painted lampshades and bedside tables have started to fade, the colours less vibrant and chipped in places. When I get up from the bed and open the dresser drawer, I'm surprised to find that the books I left behind are still here. I read the familiar titles: *Little Women, The Wind in the Willows, Black Beauty, The Secret Garden.* Some of them I read so many times the pages fell apart and I held them together with an elastic band. All the younger versions of myself still exist in this room and I can almost hear myself singing in the shower. Then I see the wrecking ball again, picture it destroying the place while I'm still inside, all the versions of me, all the versions of Norah and Laurel and Elena gone forever. What we created at the Blue Moth was nowhere near the scale and beauty and skill of Charleston, but the goal behind its creation was similar. We wanted to make our world more beautiful.

I grab my backpack and dump it out onto my bed. With an old T-shirt, I start to dust the bedside tables, chest of drawers, and the TV stand. I throw open the windows and door to air out the room. I strip the blankets off the beds and leave them in a pile by the door. With the pillows gone, the headboards are completely visible, and I trace my finger over the flowers and vines. Norah put so much effort into this design that the idea of them being destroyed is painful. I sit cross-legged on the bare mattress and just stare. Some of the colours are more vibrant than I remember, so I look closer. Between the flowers Norah has added blue moths, each one about the size of my fingernail, easily mistaken for leaves. I lean closer to the headboard to take in the detail of each moth, trying to figure out how Norah made their wings look transparent but still blue.

What are you doing? Norah says, appearing in the doorway.

We should repaint all the furniture, I say. Make it pretty again. And you should take it back to your apartment. Or maybe Laurel and Elena can take the headboards to the bungalow.

Norah crosses the room and sits next to me on the bed. She looks at the headboard and reaches out to touch one of the painted moths.

That's a good idea, she says.

The sound of the piano wafts toward us from the breakfast room and both Norah and I turn to look. It's just Puss walking across the keys, but I know Norah is thinking about those notes that pulled us across the courtyard all those years ago and changed everything.

She's still here, Norah says.

═══════════

While I was dusting furniture, the afternoon faded away and it became the golden hour. Norah and I walk along the path down to the gazebo and turn on all the battery-operated tea lights in the tissue-paper lanterns to light the way. At the firepit, Elena arranges driftwood and kindling into a triangle-shaped pile while Laurel sets up the food and drinks on a table in the gazebo. The lights hanging from the wooden beams make the gazebo glow.

Once all the tea lights are illuminated, Norah and I grab the box of fireworks and head down to the beach. We arrange them in the sand and sit on a driftwood log, looking out over the water, which is calm and inky, small waves lapping at the sand.

I'm going to go get changed, Norah says after a few minutes. She climbs the path up the bank and I stay on the beach until the sky fades from orange and pink to lilac and grey. Someone in the gazebo strums a guitar, and in the pit the fire crackles, sparks leaping into the air. We won't light the fireworks until the sky is dark, so I go join the party.

Laurel and Elena cheer when they see me crest the bank from the beach. They're each holding a beer and Elena gets me one. The bottle is dripping with condensation and makes my hand cold, but I take it and settle onto a blanket on the grass. There are fewer guests than before, some people from the far side of the island who used to stay at the Blue Moth and a few of Norah's co-workers from the bookshop. I also recognize some people from Ada's bingo nights and her famous Christmas dinners. They're all older now, and many have homes in Florida and only return to the island for the summer. It's so easy for people to fade away. I want to pull them all close, hold on to them for as long as I can. *Please stay. Don't go yet.*

I drink my beer quickly and run my hand back and forth in the grass. I know by now that the moths won't appear. It's only a story. Perhaps they never existed at all. The fire is hypnotizing, the blue flames close to the centre in sharp contrast to the yellow and orange ones shooting into the sky. In the gazebo, Laurel and Elena are dancing and I watch them for a moment. It's so easy when you're young to not see your parents as real people, to see them only in relation to yourself. But now I truly see them, finally. And they're beautiful.

As I get up to move closer to the music, I wonder what's taking Norah so long. I want her to tell the story of the moths, because she always remembers the details. But who will tell it once we're gone? And will the moths still exist if the Blue Moth Motel is reduced to rubble? I see a flash of someone coming down the lantern path. She's running, arms outstretched, wearing a blue chiffon dress. For a moment, it looks like there are two people running, a trick of the light. Then it's just Norah again and I watch as my sister takes flight, the fabric billowing around her like wings.

ACKNOWLEDGEMENTS

To my family, Emma, Tracey, and Scott, and all my extended family, thank you for putting up with my wild ideas. To Nanny Rosie, thank you for always making sure I had a book to read.

I can't fully express the extent of my gratitude to all the wonderful professors in the English department at UPEI, especially Richard Lemm and Dr. Brent MacLaine, who always encouraged me to keep writing.

To Lisa Moore and all my professors at MUN for their support and endless enthusiasm during my Master's. Lisa, I wish I had half your energy! This novel wouldn't exist without your encouragement.

To my Bookmark family, Dan, Lori, Marlene, and Adam. Working at Bookmark was and will always be my favourite job. Thank you to my PEI writing group, Keith, Chris, Rhonda, Charity, and Michelle for reading early parts of this work, as well as my St. John's writing group, Elizabeth, Beth, Terry, and Matthew, for giving wonderful feedback.

To my wonderful friends and first readers: Amy, Marsha, Emma, Hallah, Andrea, and Manrique. Without you, this book would not be what it is. Every book is a group effort, and you all participated in making this one a reality. To the Sproule family, Shanice, Lynne, Callum, and Don, thank you for opening your home to me (and Bobby!) when I had no idea what I wanted to do with my life. I can't thank you enough. My friends Robyn, Breagh, Anna, Maggie, Shanice, and Amy. My St. John's friends Nikita, Jess, Cherise, and Sam, and friends farther afield Brittani, Kirsty, Gabby, Yuni, and Carolin, thank you. Even though we don't get to see each other as much as we would like, when we do meet up it's like no time has passed at all and I'm so grateful to have you all in my life. To all my Fogo Island friends, I'm so grateful to have met you during the two summers I spent on that gorgeous island. I started this novel in a green and white saltbox house by the ocean, thanks to the Tilting Recreation and Cultural Society (TRACS), and it wouldn't exist without that amazing house.

To my Rainbow Riders family, thank you for your endless support and for making me feel so welcome. Thank you, Nathan and family, for all your support this past year. To Pam and Rob and all the other crew members here at Starship Monkstown, past and present, thank you for making St. John's feel like home. And to Puss and Boots, writing buddies extraordinaire. Their presence on my desk during the writing and editing process kept me going. Every writer should have a creature (preferably a cat!) to keep them on track.

Thank you to the Breakwater Books team, especially Rebecca Rose, Rhonda Molloy, Jocelyne Thomas, Nicole Haldoupis, and editors extraordinaire Claire Wilkshire and Sue MacLeod, for taking a chance on this little novel and helping me make it the best it can be.

And thank you to all the 2SLGBTQIA+ writers and activists. Without their work, I would not have this privileged position of being able to write a novel featuring queer characters and have it taken seriously. When I was sixteen and first decided I wanted to write a novel, I never imagined it would be a novel like this one, but I'm very glad it is.

AUTHOR PHOTO: SCOTT ROBINSON

OLIVIA ROBINSON is originally from the Annapolis Valley, Nova Scotia, and currently lives in St. John's. She completed her BA in English at UPEI and her MA in creative writing at Memorial University. Her work has appeared in *Riddle Fence, Cargo Literary Magazine,* and the *UPEI Arts Review.* In 2020, a draft of *The Blue Moth Motel* was shortlisted for the Newfoundland and Labrador Credit Union Fresh Fish Award.